choose
me

choose
me

New York Times and *USA Today* Best Selling Author

HEIDI MCLAUGHLIN

CHOOSE ME
The Archer Brothers
Book 2
© 2015 by Heidi McLaughlin

ISBN: 978-0-9906788-2-3
COVER DESIGN: Sarah Hansen at Okay Creations
EDITING: Traci Blackwood
INTERIOR DESIGN AND FORMATTING: Tianne Samson with E.M. Tippetts Book Designs

emtippettsbookdesigns.com

books by
heidi mclaughlin

The Beaumont Series

Forever My Girl Beaumont Series #1
My Everything Beaumont Series #1.5
My Unexpected Forever Beaumont Series #2
Finding My Forever Beaumont Series #3
Finding My Way Beaumont Series #4
12 Days of Forever Beaumont Series #4.5

Lost in You Series

Lost in You Lost in You #1
Lost in Us Lost in You #2

The Archer Brothers

Here With Me
Choose Me

dedication

To Those Who Fight
To Those Who Risk

We'll Never Forget

chapter 1
Nate

THE DUST SWIRLS OUT ON the plain, the wind a constant annoyance on this training exercise. Captain O'Keefe chose this location to irritate and prepare us for our Middle East deployment. I haven't been on a full deployment in a while, none of us have. Others have been getting the job done, but it's time for them to come home, decompress and spend some time with their families. Our country is at war, one that will never end and now it's our turn to go over there and do what we do best.

Tumbleweeds move toward me, on a mission to tackle me. Shooting them would make me happy, but the bullets would go nowhere and cause alarm. It's best to ignore the errant weeds because fighting with them just leaves me frustrated. The last time I moved one I drew blood from a piece of glass it had picked up on its journey.

Today, it's my duty to watch, to listen. We're going on two days with no sleep, waiting for the raid to come. Practice fighting in the desert, the smoldering heat with the sun beating down on us, is to prepare us. Knowing that at the end of this exercise I can go home, marry my girl and start the next stage in our life is a welcome relief. She's not going to like it when I tell her we're leaving again. I haven't had to deploy since my brother died. There have been a few missions here and there, but nothing that kept me away from Ryley and EJ too long.

This time will be different.

The thought of leaving Ryley and EJ for a long period of time doesn't sit well with me. It's not that she doesn't have a strong support system because she does. Lois and Carter, our best friends, will be there when she needs them. Jensen, Ryley's father, will be there to make sure EJ is doing all the father-son things that I'll miss and Carole, her mother, will make sure that Ryley is taken care of if something were to happen to me.

Ryley and I have to get married when I get back. I can't stomach the thought of knowing that I'm deploying and she and EJ won't be taken care of in the event that something happens to me. That's exactly what happened when my brother died. She found herself pregnant and alone, without any financial support. My brother should've married her when he had the chance. Instead, he left on deployment before marrying her, thinking that he was invincible and nothing would ever happen to him. Most of us have that mentality, we feel invincible. I never asked why Evan and Ryley didn't get married when they had the opportunity. I'm not willing to make the same mistakes as Evan.

Everything that occurred after his death was a nightmare for Ryley. My mother, even though I love her dearly, is the most stubborn, hardheaded and unreasonable person I know. I can understand the anger she felt, but when Evan died he didn't go away. Ryley was pregnant and giving us a piece of him that no one else could. My mother couldn't see that and still has a hard time accepting the fact that she and I are together. While she dotes on EJ, she's less than civil to Ryley and I hate that... *Evan would hate that.* My parents always loved Ryley and that shouldn't change because we choose to make a life together as a couple, as a family.

Explaining to Ryley that our time is limited won't be fun. It's certainly not a conversation starter after I've been gone for over a month. "Hey honey, I'm home for a few weeks." A few weeks… the thought of what we have to do in that time both excites and depresses me all at once. A rush wedding, sad goodbye's and hopefully a baby conceived. I'll have maybe a day or two before I have to break the news to her.

My radio crackles, causing me to cock my head to the side to listen. Nothing follows, there's no command, just radio static. Someone is warning us that our mission is underway even though they shouldn't because the intent is to catch us off-guard. Still, the warning is welcomed. It's been forty-eight hours out in this desert and I'm ready to go home. All we have to do is complete this exercise and we're on our way back.

Looking through my scope I spot an armadillo walking across the plain. The wind and heat makes everything shimmer causing me to blink and refocus. My spotter, Texas, is next to me. He chuckles, likely wondering if I'm going to blast the critter or let him keep walking.

"He could be dinner," he mumbles under his breath. His real name is Carl Poole, but he earned the nickname Texas when he showed up at a gathering with shit kickers, a cowboy hat and a piece of straw hanging out of his mouth. He solidified his handle when he asked if we all wanted to go to a hoedown. SEALs spend a lot of time together and know just about everything about each other. The day we left he found out that his sometimes girlfriend is pregnant. We wanted to celebrate that night, but he said he wasn't sure it was his baby because he hadn't been with her in a few months. Tex will do the right thing, and I know Ryley will help his girlfriend while we're deployed. It's all part of being a family.

"I hear the meat is tough." I try to adjust my position, one that I've been in for hours waiting for a sign that we're on. Peering through my scope again, there's nothing. We've been here for over a month and I have yet to fire my rifle. We sit and wait. We talk and strategize. We go over images of mountain ranges and terrain. This is not my idea of a training mission, but rather a slumber party with the g-rated version of Rambo.

"We're done," Tex says after his radio squawks. He starts packing up, putting our gear back into our packs.

"What are you talking about?" I ask, incredulously. We've been out here for two days, for what? I remain in position, in case this is a set-up and an ambush is coming.

Tex shrugs. "Dunno. Command says break down and come in."

I look around for any sign that Tex could be wrong, but see nothing amiss. This exercise doesn't make sense and seems more and more like a waste of time. We could've been home with our families, giving them a proper goodbye instead of being out here.

"What the fuck?" I yell as I stand and sling my rifle over my shoulder. I'm not letting go for fear that this is a trap. It wouldn't be the first time a set-up has happened and caught us off guard.

By the time I'm packed, Tex is waiting. He seems anxious

to get back to camp. I'm willing to bet that his girl has called and he's eager to speak to her. Ryley won't call. It's something she used to do for Evan, but won't do it for me. I don't blame her, she had to make some changes in her life and she mostly changed anything that had to do with Evan.

As soon as we arrive back at camp, the MH-60 SpecOps variant Black Hawk lands to take us back to base. As I look around, it's clear that this place has been cleaned up and our bags packed for us.

"You comin'?" Tex asks as he shoulders his bag. I nod, but don't move. Something isn't right about this whole situation. We should've had a weapons check and gone over our exercise. We should've sat down and dissected every movement of our enemy until we had everything memorized. We spent all this time out here, and for what – to look at maps?

Tex bumps my shoulder as he walks by. He stops and waits for me.

"Yeah," I tell him as I reach for my bags. "Something isn't right," I mutter to myself as I walk out toward our waiting transport.

chapter 2
Evan

THIS IS HOW LIFE IS supposed to be... my son on my hip, my dog at my feet and my beautiful girl standing in front of me dripping wet because I've just dumped her into the ocean. EJ laughs in my arms, and my heart swells with pride and admiration for this little boy. I know he's part me, but I wasn't here for so many milestones in his life – from the first time he kicked, to when he was born, to taking his first steps. I've missed so much. All for a job I love that doesn't love me back.

"Look," EJ says, as he points to sky. A kite in the shape of a bird flies above us. The closer it comes to us, the larger the shadow it makes. I use this opportunity to stare at Ryley as she watches the animated bird. Waves crash around her legs, and she wobbles a little. I should move, go stand by her, but I'm lost in her beauty. From the first day I saw her, I knew she was the one. She's my angel, my saving grace... but she's also my destruction. She could end my world by telling me that she wants to be with Nate and there won't be anything I can do about it. As she stands in front of me, with the sun shining down and encasing her, I can't even begin to comprehend how lucky I am to be with her right now.

After I returned home, standing there on the porch with my cap in my hand and seeing her look at me with such horror in her eyes, I didn't understand. I couldn't understand. When she told me that I was dead and cautiously touched me as if I wasn't real, I thought I had lost her. There was no way to understand the words coming out of her mouth. Her face streaked with tears and her voice laced with anger brought me to my knees. What had happened over the years to cause this and why? And how was I going to get her back and make things right?

Fight, that's how.

This fight to win her back, to keep her as my own, is going to be the death of me. It's a fight I won't be giving up unless there's a bullet in my head, or she tells me to leave. I know in my heart that she loves me. It's my mind that refuses to let go of the images of her and my brother together. Thinking about him touching her, knowing that he's wanted her since we were teens is the nail in my proverbial coffin. And where is he now? The storm rolls in and he's conveniently gone. His crew is on an abruptly scheduled training mission. He *has* to know I'm back. He's *had* to have been called. So why isn't he home?

Ryley splashes me, causing EJ to squirm in my arms. I set him down and watch him run to her. She scoops him up in her arms, just like you see in those cheesy romantic comedies that she watches. I don't want to be on the outside looking in, but I can't pressure her. The decision she made the other night, saying she wasn't going to marry Nate, made my heart soar but also caused me to take pause. They've built a life without me, a life that has my son calling my brother "Dad", and left me to be nothing more to him than the guy whose face is on his walls.

Thinking about my son and him not knowing me the way he should angers me. Ryley and Nate were wrong on so many levels, and I'm not sure that's something I can ever forgive. Growing up, we were close to our uncles and that's what I always envisioned Nate being to my children. EJ should've known from day one that *I* was his father, dead or alive. I earned that moniker, Nate didn't.

"What are you thinking so hard about?"

A half smile forms on my lips and by the look in her eyes she knows my mind is up to no good. I should tell her how angry I am, but each day with her is a blessing right now and I don't want to ruin what few moments we have together.

"Just thinking about how beautiful you are, standing there holding our son." Ryley's cheeks turn a glorious shade of pink as she sets her forehead against EJ's shoulder.

"I think you're biased."

I shrug. I know I'm not. She's gorgeous and always has been. I'm not the only one who thinks this. "Doesn't matter if I am, it's the truth. I'm willing to bet your father gave you a similar compliment the first time he saw you holding EJ."

Ryley walks toward me with EJ still in her arms. When she's shoulder to shoulder with me, she pauses. "You've missed so much." Her comment knocks me back and she doesn't give me an opportunity to speak or defend myself.

I didn't want to miss anything, but that freedom was ripped from me. My ability to choose to call home was taken as if I were a common criminal. Missing time in their lives was not a part of any plan of mine. I was doing my job.

I turn and watch her walk back up the beach with EJ still looking over at me. Deefur follows behind just like he's supposed to. I'm sure there's a reason why I missed everything and I'm going to figure it out. Whatever that reason is, I'll never be able to make it up to Ryley and EJ. Nothing will ever bring back the time that was missed, the years and milestones.

It's not just EJ or Ryley who have suffered from me being gone. I've suffered as well, but not nearly to the extent they have. Even though I had the pictures and letters, which were clearly forged, I still had *something*. They had nothing. My family was left with a box of my possessions and pictures of me. They were told to grieve and move on while I was fighting for some cause that I'm not even sure was valid.

The sand is hot and quickly sticks to my feet as I walk back toward our blanket. EJ is in front of Ryley building a sand castle, his shovel digging ferociously in the sand. I dodge a few flying clumps the closer I get to him.

"Can you help me, Eban?" I crouch down and move his hair out of his eyes.

"Let me talk to your mom for a minute and then I'll be right here to help, okay?"

"K," he says without making eye contact, far too busy with his masterpiece. I stay there, crouched down, and watch him for a moment before making my way to the blanket. Ryley closes her book when I sit down, pulling her knees to her chest. This is her way of protecting herself. I noticed this habit shortly after we started dating, but never thought anything of it until I told her I enlisted. That's when it dawned on me that she's putting up a wall -- one that I've taken down repeatedly and will do so again and again if need be.

"You know I can read you like an open book."

"You forget that I can do the same. You were thinking about something that upset you." Her voice is soft and quiet as she keeps her attention focused on EJ. I reach beneath her arm and pull her hand into mine. I want to touch her, hold her, while I can. There's a feeling in the pit of stomach warning me this bubble we've been in is about to burst.

"You were standing there, holding our son, and all I could think about is how he doesn't know I'm his dad and he should. He should've known from day one that I was his dad whether I was here or not."

"You're right," she says quickly, surprising me. I expected we'd sit in silence while she mentally berated herself. "I was young and stupid and thinking with a broken heart. I couldn't believe that our child, the one we wanted and loved before he was even here, wouldn't know his father. When I was told that you had... that you weren't coming back I told myself I would do this by myself and I did. I delivered him in a room with just the doctor and his staff. No one held my hand, but I thought you did. I know now that it was crazy to think you were in the room with me.

"When EJ started talking and really recognizing who people were, he started saying 'dada' and I didn't think anything of it until he called Nate 'Daddy' and I didn't have the heart to tell him not to do that. He had playgroups and daycare so he saw his friends doing the same thing. Nate would pick him up sometimes and it was natural for EJ to say it."

Ryley looks at me with tears in her eyes. "I hate myself for allowing it to happen, but I can't take it back. You can hate me because of it, but you can't hate EJ or Nate. Nate only did what I asked of him."

I pull her into my arms and kiss the top of her head. "I could never hate you, Ry. I love you more than anything. But you can't ask me not to hate Nate. I'll never forgive him for what he's done."

Ryley raises her head and stares me down. "I did things, too."

Leaning forward, I kiss the tip of her nose. "Yes, but there's a code between brothers and he broke it."

chapter 3
Nate

MY EYES JAR OPEN AS soon as we land. I can't believe I actually dozed off. It's unlike me not to remain alert and focused, especially when I have so much on my mind. I can't get this nagging suspicion out of my system that something is up. The training mission, in my opinion, was a waste of time. Aside from going over maps of the Middle East and places we've all been, we didn't train. We lounged around like useless slugs. That's not how we win the battle. That's not how we defeat the enemy. They're not sitting around waiting, and the more I think about it, the more pissed off I get.

Stepping off the helo, I breathe in the sea air of Coronado. I love it here. Growing up in Washington, the constant rain and gray is what I was used to but once I moved south, I realized that seeing the sun every day is what I needed.

I wouldn't trade where I am for anything. The last time I re-enlisted I feared being assigned to a different base and I'm not sure what I would've done if that had happened because there would've been no way I'd leave Ryley and EJ behind. Asking Ryley to leave is out of the question. Evan is buried here and I already know what her answer would be.

"Plans for the day?" Tex asks as we walk to the bus. He has a shit eating grin on his face, pretty much indicating that he's up to something.

"Depending on what time this debriefing is done, I'll probably go home and sit on the couch with Ryley on one side and EJ on the other."

"York said no debriefing today, don't need it." He drops his gear onto the bus and walks away. I stop dead in my tracks, unsure if I heard him correctly. I look around for York, but I don't see him. Mark York is our Master Chief, divorced with two kids that he doesn't get to see much. Since his divorce he tends to keep to himself and rarely hangs out with us. He was, and probably still is in love with his ex and the fact that she took his kids back to her home state has really put his life in perspective. He talks about retirement, but re-enlisted a few months back saying that the SEALs are the only thing keeping him going.

York is ready for deployment, so is Tex. I'm not. Ryley and I need more time before I ship off. She's always on edge right before I have to leave. It's even worse when I leave without much notice. My idea of a honeymoon doesn't consist of leaving my bride and son days after we get married but I know it happens to all of us. It's the military version of a shotgun wedding, a way of life...

Country first.

I get my gear stowed and climb onto the bus. It's a short trip across base to our training facility. I honestly feel like running back, yet another component to a busted training exercise. I'm not tired even though I should be. I close my eyes and rest my head against the window of the bus. It's the only way I can shut my brain off. I picture what it's going to be like when I get home. EJ will be out back playing on his swing set with Deefur standing guard. Ryley will be weeding her flower garden, picking and pruning to keep her roses alive. Far off in the distance, in between planes taking off, the ocean will crash against the beach giving me a subtle reminder that we need to take a trip down there. I'm going to stand there, taking them all in before I announce that I'm home.

My eyes spring open as I lurch forward when the driver slams on his brakes. My eyes weren't closed for ten minutes, and yet it felt like an hour. I scrub my hands over my face and wait my turn to get off. Tex stops in front of me, giving me a pass.

"You slept on the plane and the bus. You're not getting old on me are you?"

"Nah, I was just resting my eyes."

"Cold feet?" he asks, laughing.

"Hell no," I say as I shoulder my rucksack. "There's something not sitting right with that training mission and not having a debriefing."

"What the hell would we debrief, the life of an armadillo by Tex and Arch? It was a busted training exercise. Maybe they'll push our deployment back because of it. Who knows, just be happy you're home and you get to marry that fine looking babe of yours." Tex definitely has a way of putting everything in perspective. That or he just doesn't care. He has his own things to worry about with his girl being pregnant. He's afraid of making a commitment to her and finding out the kid isn't his.

Tex is everything you'd expect in a cowboy but not a SEAL. Yet, there isn't another man I'd trust as much to have beside me in battle, with the exception of my teammates. When Tex arrived on base he was this toothpick-looking kid. I had seen him around, but never gave him more than a friendly 'hi'. He tested for the SEALs a year after, having put on a considerable amount of weight and muscle. He was top of his class, deadly with a rifle and a damn fine warrior.

Once my gear is back in my locker, I'm in my truck and heading home. No one lingers when you don't have to unless there's something brewing, then it's pow-wow time. Only a few from my team live off base like I do. I broached the subject of moving to the Naval Station with Ryley after we get married, but she shot me down. It was stupid on my part, knowing that Evan bought them the house. It was my failed attempt to move past his death and on with our lives. Sometimes, I think it's unhealthy to live there. Granted, all his stuff is gone – packed up in boxes being stored in the attic - but his ghost is there. Many times I'll catch her just staring at the mantle. I do it too, but for different reasons.

One minor detour and I find myself where I hadn't planned on going, at least not today. Ryley and EJ are waiting for me, and yet here I am walking through the grass with my hands stuffed into the pockets of my camo pants. I kneel down and wipe a few fallen leaves away from Evan's marker.

Choose Me

EVAN ARCHER

SOC US NAVY
SEAL TEAM III
Son, Brother, Friend
Proud to Serve

Nowhere does it say anything about being a boyfriend, fiancé or a father. My mother did this, driving an even bigger wedge between us. She said it was tacky adding that he was a fiancé and especially a father when he wasn't. It didn't matter how hard I fought, I couldn't get her to change her mind. Evan wouldn't have wanted his marker to be like this.

"Shit's crazy, man," I say out loud. I want others to hear me, especially those who don't get visitors. I may be here to talk to my brother, but the other guys buried here can listen.

"I've been gone for over a month training for deployment and we didn't fire our guns once. We sat out in the desert and contemplated the life of tumbleweeds. I don't know…" I pause and look around. There are a few people here, wives mostly. "We didn't debrief either. Seems odd and I can't shake the feeling that something's up."

I sit down, pulling my knees up and resting my hands over them. "I can't imagine how much EJ has changed since I've been gone. I hate leaving them, Evan, but she tells me to go. I thought about taking a desk job. You know, asking Carole for a recommendation or something, but I wouldn't be happy and Ryley knows that. I'm deploying soon. I just found out and have to tell her when I get home. I don't even want to see the look on her face, or to tell EJ that I have to go away for eighteen months.

"This war, it's ugly. We're fighting and when we think we've made headway, another group pops up and everything we've accomplished seems to be thrown to the wayside. They don't care about their country or their families. They only care about hurting people and destruction.

"Livvie and Mom are doing okay. I just wish things were different. Getting Mom to accept anything is like taking candy from a two year old. It's sad, but I'm not even looking forward to telling her that I'm leaving. I don't care if she comes down to say goodbye or not, because when she's here she stresses Ryley out and I do enough of that for the both of us.

"While I was gone, I started thinking back to high school. Life was so much easier and our biggest worry was any upcoming game we had or making sure we didn't track mud into the house. Sometimes I want to go back to those days and pretend that 9-11 didn't happen, and that we didn't change our course. Losing you and Dad, both in combat, it makes me stop and think. I love my country, but I love my family too and sometimes I think they should come first.

"EJ will be starting school this year. He's a walking, talking mini version of you. I think he'll enlist when he's older, and that scares me. Ryley doesn't say anything, but I know she's thinking about it. I don't remember playing 'Army' when we were kids. I don't know, maybe we did. He does it all the time because it's what he knows. Maybe before I go home I'll get him a destroyer and teach him to play Battleship, steer him on the right path if he's going to enlist. I just can't lose him, too. He's my last link to you and Dad and I don't know what I'd do without him in my life."

I lie back in the grass with my arms behind my head. Evan and I did this once after our father died. We stayed with him the night he was buried so he wouldn't be alone. When the sun rose that next morning, I realized that I had never closed my eyes.

When Evan died, I didn't leave for a week.

"Losing you, Evan, changed everything."

chapter 4
Evan

A FEW MORE BEACHGOERS ARRIVE as bonfires are started and music is played. I sit next to Ryley while EJ plays a few feet in front of us. Deefur lies next to him watching his every move. Deefur has turned out to be the dog I thought he would be, a protector and best friend. The sun, still blazing and far from setting, keeps us shrouded in daylight. It's almost a perfect day if only life wasn't looming over us. There's still the ongoing uncertainty of what's going to happen to us and finding out how everything went to shit when we went on that mission.

I can't keep putting off my own investigation. River says we should wait, but waiting only gives the people at the top more time to bury the truth. He's the luckiest of us all. His wife never thought he was dead, or she just lived in denial. When he arrived home, he was welcomed with open arms while the rest of us struggled. There's still the matter of our other team members and why only four of us were sent on the mission.

Far too many questions linger without enough answers.

Ryley leans her head on my shoulder and I slouch down to make her more comfortable. Being on the beach, it's as if we're the only people in the world that exist. It's as if the moment we start packing up and heading to the car, reality shines like a high wattage flashlight right in our path, reminding us that we can't see what's coming. Nate. Finding out what happened to us. Learning who's responsible. They're all catalysts for our destruction.

Deefur adjusts to sitting and stares at the kids down the beach. His growl is just loud enough to alert me that he doesn't like something. I look around, trying to be as subtle as I can. Ryley doesn't hear Deefur or she'd say something. Nothing looks out of the ordinary, but that doesn't mean my senses aren't heightened. Dogs are great at signaling when something isn't right.

"EJ," I yell. He turns his head, looking at me over his shoulder. "Why don't you build this way? You're getting too far."

"Okay, Eban." And just like that he turns toward us and starts his digging adventure. Deefur cocks his head slightly, alternating between looking down the beach and watching EJ before turning his focus back on the people not too far from us.

Eban. Him saying my name instead of "Dad" or "Daddy" makes me think. I'm waiting for Ryley to say something, but I'm not sure how long I'm willing to wait. I'm his father, dead or not. He needs to know the truth, and it's better now than later.

"Should we think about heading home?" I'm reluctant to leave, but Deefur has me on edge.

"No, home is messy. The beach is serene and calm. Besides, EJ is having fun and we're here as a family. Why do you want to go home?"

I can't tell her that the dog has me concerned and that he thinks that there's a threat here. I don't want her to panic. The other night was enough. After spending time with River, Frannie, Rask and McCoy, we're all on edge. There's a fear we all carry. Someone doesn't want us alive and they know we're not going to stop until we figure out why. That puts our families in danger, and causes a lot of sleepless nights for me.

Shrugging, I try to play it off. Truth is, I want to pack her and EJ up and head to Washington for a while. I'd like to visit some of my father's old Navy buddies and see if they can help. I figured the retired vets who are still working might have a better chance at uncovering something even though I know Carole is going to use her resources. I can't let Ryley's mom risk her career or her life for me.

I kiss Ryley on the head and stand, a ruse so I can change positions without having to ask her to move. I sit behind her and she immediately falls into my arms.

"Are you cold?" I ask as she pulls her long sleeves over her hands.

She shakes her head. "No, I just got a chill. It's passed now." Ryley rests her head on my arm and her back against my chest. This is perfection. At least it is for me.

"I've been meaning to talk to you about Livvie moving in. I know you said it's fine, but you also said she and my mother haven't treated you very well since my…" I can't bring myself to say the word *death* out loud. Being gone for six years is nothing compared to hearing that your family thinks you're dead. "If you're not comfortable with her being there, I'll ask her to leave."

Ryley sighs. "She's good with EJ."

I lean forward as far as I can to make eye contact with her. "But is she good with you? I don't want things at the house to be awkward," I tell her as I lean back and pull her to my chest. "You need to be comfortable in your home and if she makes you uncomfortable, I'll ask her to leave. I'm sure she has friends down here, or she can stay with Carter and Lois."

Ryley nods and her hands hang from my arms. "Lois would love that. Grace loves Livvie."

"Who's Grace?"

She chuckles lightly. "Grace is EJ's future wife." I tickle her sides when she says that and continue to do so even as she attempts to move away from me.

"You know he may be a boy, but no woman will ever be good enough for him," I say once I let go. Ryley crawls back into her spot and faces me.

"I feel the same way and I know your mom does as well. Thing is, when you fall in love, it's because of who you're meant to be with, not who your parents choose for you." Her hand caresses my face and I fight every urge to lean in and steal a kiss. "Grace is Carter and Lois's daughter. She's just a few months younger than EJ."

Taking her hand from my cheek, I kiss her palm. "You and Lois were pregnant together." I say matter-of-factly. "When we were in high school I remember Carter coming over one day all freaked out because Lois thought she was pregnant and all I could think about was what it would be like to see you holding our child. I was eighteen and having thoughts about us having a family. That day in the park, when I hit you – which I'm thinking wasn't an accident at all but actually kismet – I knew then that you were meant for me, Ry."

With the strict *no kissing in front of EJ* policy in place, she wraps her arms around me. I want to lay her down and hold her, but won't compromise her like that in front of EJ. There's so much I want to do to her, but can't. My hands are furtively tied behind my back where she's concerned and I know I'm going to lose my shit if I see Nate touch her.

She pulls away, resuming her spot between my legs. She brings my arms around her, encasing her. "We need to talk about what happens when Nate comes back."

There's a low growl building when she brings up his name and pending return. I'm not looking forward to seeing him act as if he's me. He's taken my girl, my son, my dog and my house and if he thinks that I'm just going to walk away gracefully, he's got another think coming. Ryley is the only one who can tell me to leave and I don't think she will.

"I'm not going to pretend I know what I'm doing, but EJ can't get hurt. Nate is going to come home soon, and whether you like it or not, he thinks of that house as his home. When he does… when you see him, you can't hurt him. You can't fight, not in front of EJ."

"I want to kill him, Ry."

She turns, facing me with tears in her eyes. Again, her hand caresses my cheek. "You won't because your son loves him."

I look at EJ, so innocent and unaware of the truth, a truth that he needs to know. If Ryley and Nate think I'm going to stand by and let this charade continue, they're sorely mistaken. Children are resilient. That's something I learned from the mission we were on. Each child we saved gave us hope even though they had none themselves.

Ryley brings my face back to hers. "Are you hearing me?"

"I want my family back, Ryley." I leave her with that thought, and go back over to EJ as I had promised earlier. I start helping him build his sand castle, working together as father and son.

chapter 5
Nate

COMING HOME TO AN EMPTY house is not my idea of happiness. I've been counting the hours until I could return home... until I could hold Ryley and play ball with EJ in the backyard. At this point, mowing the lawn is better than where I've been. I'm just happy to be home.

The house has an eerie feel, almost somber. It's too quiet for my liking. I turn on the TV to create some background noise. The luggage in the corner catches my eye and I rifle through it. I'm nosey. It's my nature. It's full of women's clothing but nothing Ryley would wear. Maybe Carter and Lois had a fight while I was gone and she's been staying here. I doubt it, but it's better than thinking Ryley has suddenly taken on a transient.

I walk into the kitchen and pull a beer out of the fridge. I should call Ryley and tell her I'm home, but I think surprising her would be best. I love seeing the look on her face when I come home. The way she feels pressed against my body after

I've been gone. I've missed her terribly and need to hold her.

Sitting down on the couch, I pick up the pad of paper on the coffee table, hoping to find a note as to where she might be. It's just her doodles, the silly little drawings that she used to do back in high school.

She draws swirly designs all over her notepad. I don't know why girls do this. Is it so they don't have to make eye contact with us? If so, that's the stupidest reason ever. She didn't even move when I sat down. I saw her in the hall earlier and almost lost my shit. Evan is going to freak out when he finds out. I send him a quick text, letting him know that the angel that saved him from purgatory is sitting next to me in class. I sort of want to ask her to look at me so I can razz him later about the shiner he gave her. I've never seen him so pussy whipped by a girl he doesn't even know.

I wish I could remember her name. If I did, I could introduce myself again. I wasn't paying attention yesterday because I thought she was just another piece of ass for Evan. But he acted differently around her at the park, and I've never seen him stare at the phone for so long. That's where I found him this morning – asleep with his head on top of the phone. He had a nice indent when he woke up.

She peers at me, and I smile. She probably thinks I'm creepy. I probably am creepy. Her head pops up and now she's full on staring. I close my mouth, afraid that I have something in my teeth. Evan has been making me drink those damn protein shakes in the morning to bulk up, but I know I brushed my teeth. There can't be any residue left, right?

"You look just like your brother," she blurts out and I'm rewarded with the most glorious shade of red as she blushes. Her beautiful hair -- the color of red autumn leaves -- tries to hide her face, and I'm tempted to reach out and push it behind her ear.

Wait, what?
This is Evan's girl.
I can't touch her.

But I want to.

I laugh, and it's awkward. She turns to face me again and her eyes pierce mine. She thinks I'm laughing at her. I'm not. I'm laughing at my idiotic heart that is falling for a girl my brother desperately wants. Oh, the irony.

"We're twins, and you just made the other me very happy." Where do I come up with this crap? We're twins? And why do I care if he's happy? I want her for myself. Maybe she'll see just how much of a douche Evan can be and I can console her.

She clears her throat and faces the front. I want her to turn and stare at me so I can form the perfect picture tonight before going to bed. I want to memorize every inch of her porcelain face and hold her delicate hands in mine. I want to protect her from the world.

I turn away when she glances at me. I shouldn't have these feelings but I can't help it. Evan's right, she's an angel. But if she's the angel, he most certainly is the devil and I know I'll have to bide my time until he's moved on. I'll be there to mend her broken heart even if the wait kills me.

Evan texts back asking me if I'm serious. I could lie, but that will only work until he sees her himself. She's new; everyone will be talking about her. I can't hide her as much as I'd love to.

"Evan has been pacing by the phone waiting for you to call. He's going to be outside that door when the bell rings now that he knows you're here."

She looks at the door and back at me. Her expression is stoic. Her hands clutch the end of her desk, and her knuckles turn white.

"What was your name again?" I ask my tongue thick in my throat.

"Ryley Clarke." Her voice is barely above a whisper but it's enough to make the hairs on my arm stand tall.

"What's yours?"

I like that she cares even if she's just returning the gesture.

"Nate. Nate Archer." This is my opportunity to touch her so I

extend my hand for her to shake. I feel my eyes go wide when we shake hands. "Like I said, Evan will be very happy to see you." I want to add that she should run in the opposite direction and that I'll be there to meet her. I'm the good one of the both of us. Not him.

My heart races the closer the second hand gets to the bell. I wish I had never sent that text and just talked to her myself. What harm would that have done? I could've easily told Evan I forgot what she looked like. He wouldn't have bought it since he spent the night reciting everything that he loved about her. I know once he gets her into the backseat of his car he'll be done with her. I won't mind. I can't fight what my heart wants.

The bell signals the end of class and Mr. Reed throws his pen onto his desk and waves the students out. It's only the first day and he already looks flustered. I gather my things slowly and walk down the aisle staying one step behind Ryley. I'm trying not to watch her, but I can't help it.

I let her go in front of me and as soon as we're both facing the door, I see Evan. His head is bent slightly and he's watching her like a hawk watches his prey. When Donna, his weekly "friend" walks by, I expect he'll start watching her, but her presence doesn't faze him. That doesn't bode well for me.

I hate my brother right now. The coolness oozes off him. I didn't get the sex appeal gene. I got the brains. Why can't I have both? He beckons her with his finger and she goes, just like every other girl in this school. He looks up, catches me watching and shakes his head. He's telling me she's off limits.

I don't wait to see what happens next. I put my head down and walk to my locker, letting the regret build with each step I take.

I should've never texted him.

Footsteps bound up the front porch steps. I place my beer on the table and smile at the memory of the first day I met Ryley. Everything could've been different but like I predicted, I was here to pick up the pieces when Evan died. It's not how

I wanted things to be with us, but I'll take whatever I can get.

The front door opens and Ryley walks in. She's laughing and looking behind her. She doesn't know I'm here, reminding me that we need to talk about security and her being cautious when I'm not home. I see the top of EJ's head, knowing instantly that someone is carrying him. He's being held too high up for it to be Lois holding him.

They step in and all eyes are on me. My throat closes as we stand there, staring at each other. I blink, closing my eyes tightly and pray that when I open them again all I will see are Ryley and EJ standing before me.

When I open them my worst nightmare has come true. A ghost is holding my son – the boy I've raised. A man I buried years ago stands before me, having just been laughing with my fiancée a moment ago.

I look from him to Ryley and back. I don't even want to think about what's been going on or how the hell he ended up in our living room.

"Daddy!" EJ exclaims, and the only solace I feel right now is running toward me after being set down. I scoop him up and look at my dead brother as he eyes me with his newly found possession.

"How are you here?" I ask, clearly in shock.

"Ah, don't act so surprised little brother. It's not like you didn't know I was alive."

I didn't.

chapter 6
Evan

I HAVEN'T SEEN MY BROTHER in six years. We haven't spoken or emailed. It's not because we were angry at each other – although he might be now that I'm standing in front of him – it's because I've been fighting against an enemy that may or may not be some type of cover up. Little did I know that I'd also be fighting to get my family back from the one person I trusted to keep them safe.

He stands here, holding my son in his arms as if nothing has happened. As if I'm the one who doesn't belong here in my own home. The one *I* bought with Ryley and *we* had planned to fix up together. He's said nothing to combat the accusation that I believe is true – he knew what was going on. Instead, he ignores me and doesn't even seem shocked that I've miraculously "come back from the dead".

Nate sets EJ down and kisses him on top of his head. "Go upstairs, EJ. I need to talk to Mommy about work stuff."

"But what about yous tellin' me about your trip?"

"I promise, I will," Nate is soft and gentle with my son, his fingers linger on EJ's cheek, and his eyes tell me that he loves my boy.

"Can you tell me later?"

"Yeah, I'll be up."

EJ hangs on every word Nate says and holds his hand up for a high-five when he passes by. "Later Eban."

My own voice is caught in my throat. My son has just dismissed me because he believes his father is home. I am home, yet I don't belong. My brother needs to say something. He needs to face me like a man. There's a bond between brothers, twins especially, that is hard to sever. Our bond was strengthened when we joined the Navy together, when we became SEALs together. Nothing should come between us, but we both know Ryley and EJ will, and for good reason. Our mother and sister will divide the family because of all of this, taking unnecessary sides, sides that were created by Nate for his own benefit.

If something happened to me while on a mission, he should've found out what went wrong and why. SEALs are the elite of elite, the best of the best. We don't turn our backs and pretend like everything is okay. We fight until the end. We protect our family.

We don't covet.

When Nate and I were little, we fought, but never anything too serious - he would take a toy from me, or vice versa. I'm older by five minutes and I've never let him forget it. I matured faster, shaved first and had a girlfriend before he did. He studied harder, worked out longer and always stayed after practice to be better. With siblings there's always competition, but with twins I think it's worse.

The one thing I could always count on is that Nate would have my back, just as I would have his. People knew not to mess with the Archer twins because where there's one, his brother isn't far behind. We knew we could always count on each other. The same thing went with Ryley, who was my first serious girlfriend. Once I met her, everyone paled in comparison. Nate protected her like a sister… a *sister*. So right now when I look at Nate living in my home, sleeping with my girl and raising my son, all I see is anger. He's deceived me for years. I knew he liked her, but I never thought he'd do what he's done.

It's one thing to be a father figure to my son, hell I would've done the same thing, but I would've never crossed the line with his fiancée.

To me, that is unforgivable.

He needs to be a man and admit that he capitalized on my absence so he could take Ryley away from me. Part of me wishes our lives didn't come to this because after being gone so long, all I want to do is sit back and enjoy my time home. That includes catching a game or two with my brother, who up until this past month was my best friend.

"So how'd it happen?" I ask, knowing that if he goes into details about how he and Ryley ended up together it's going to make my stomach turn, but needing to hear it from him anyway.

Nate shakes his head and before I can say anything the soft touch of her hand is on my arm. "That's an unfair question, Evan, and you know it."

She's right, but I'm giving neither of them the satisfaction of knowing I agree with her. The anger I felt for Ryley is back now that Nate is home. His posture and relaxed state tells me everything I believe to be true. He must have known and did nothing about it. He took advantage of a cover-up to pursue his own twisted fantasy and make it a reality.

"Do you have anything to say?"

Nate looks at me and his eyes drift down to where Ryley is touching my arm. She removes her hand and it doesn't take a rocket scientist to figure out that she did that for his benefit. I look at her, her eyes are downcast and she's staring at the floor. I shake my head at the thought that everything we've worked for these past few weeks is now circling down the drain.

"Everything is so awkward." Ryley's voice is low, but crystal clear. I want to shake her, ask her if she thought that Nate was going to disappear for the next six years so she wouldn't be faced with this decision.

"Awkward?" I question. "You think this is *awkward*? How the hell do you think I feel right now?" She jumps back, causing Nate to stand. I look at him and point. "You don't get to protect her right now. You knew where I was, Nate, and you did nothing. I know for a fact that there wasn't a damn thing in the press about how or where we died. Just that four SEALs came home dead.

"You say you identified my body but how the hell could you not know it wasn't me? I'm your fucking twin for God's sake. Everything that runs through my veins runs through yours."

I stop and turn away from them, my hands clenching at my sides. The anger soaring through my body right now is enough to cause physical damage, but I can't with EJ in the house. The therapy sessions haven't prepared me for this confrontation and I know I'm not supposed to lay blame, but I can't help it. Doc Howard believes that there's been a cover-up and everything appears to indicate the same, but I can't get over the fact that my own brother believed that I was dead.

"We've all struggled with this news, Evan. But I don't think Nate knew you were alive. He would've gone after you."

Why is she protecting him? Does she love him so much that she can't see he's always pined after her? That this was the perfect opportunity for him to take my place in her life? To pretend that he's me when he watches her close her eyes at night.

"Are you changing your mind about us, Ryley?" I turn and face them both.

I get a small sense of victory when I ask that question and see Nate's face fall. He looks at her and his eyes beg her to tell him I'm wrong.

"Ryley?" she refuses to look at him. I should feel like shit. I should have some remorse for breaking him like this, but I don't. He's taken the one person I love and tried to make her love him instead.

"I don't know," she says meekly, avoiding eye contact with either of us. My head shakes as I bite the inside of my cheek.

"Seriously, Ry?" I ask, even more pissed off than I was before. "What about —"

"Not now, Evan," she says sternly. Her eyes are like daggers as they pierce through me, tearing apart what little we had started to rebuild.

"I see."

"No, you don't. All you see is that Nate is home and we're engaged. You see me, right now, but you don't see me the way I need you to." Ryley angles her body so she's facing me, tears rolling down her face. "For years I battled through the pain of losing you and so did Nate. I didn't set out to be with him, and he knows that. You were dead. We buried you, and yes there was a mistake, but we can't erase the damage that has been done. We have to move forward and you have to have patience with both me and EJ."

Ryley wipes angrily at her cheeks, smearing her tears. "And you," she says, facing Nate. "If you knew your brother was alive, I'll never forgive you. If this was some ploy or some act to be with me —"

"Ryley, why would you think that?" Nate's voice is pleading, and I realize it's probably how mine sounded too.

"I don't know, but the thoughts are there, Nate. How could no one know they were alive? How could you have identified his body?"

Nate takes a deep breath. "Your face was mangled." He looks at me as he says this. "Your arms were missing, so there weren't any tattoos and I couldn't match our birthmarks. Believe me that's the first thing I looked for. They told me that a bomb had gone off and they had recovered as much of you as possible. They showed me your dog tags and a picture of Ryley from high school, that's all there was. I asked for a DNA test and they swabbed my cheek right there. A few days later it came back as a match."

"Did you ever think it was your own DNA?" I ask.

"No, not until you walked through the door. I trusted them. Why wouldn't I?"

"We *all* trusted them," I correct him as I pull my tags out from under my shirt. "But that doesn't excuse you from taking over my life."

35

chapter 7
Nate

I DIDN'T KNOW.

I didn't know.

I didn't know.

I repeat the same three words over and over again in my head while Evan blatantly glares at me. I can't keep my eyes fixed on him, even though the warrior in me is telling me not to break eye contact. My eyes shift from him to Ryley and back again, trying to piece together what's been going on since I left, or since Evan returned from the dead.

"Daddy, are you coming?"

Evan turns sharply at the sound of EJ calling for me. His jaw tightens. His fists are clenched. I can't blame him, but I'm not correcting EJ and neither has Ryley. Evan may be his biological father, but I'm his dad. I've raised him since he was born. I've been there through every illness, bump, scrape and I've earned the right to be bearer of the title. But as I look at my brother and *my* fiancée standing in front me, together, I'm not sure that'll be enough.

"I'll be up in a minute, buddy," my voice cracks as I call up to EJ. He's the one who is going to suffer the most. The adults can push everything under the rug and move on, but EJ is too little to understand. He's not going to be able to grasp the difference between Evan and myself.

And I refuse to tell EJ I'm not his dad.

"Are you going to answer me, or just stand there?" Evan moves to sit down, crossing his leg over his knee like him being here is no big deal, when it in fact, it's monumental. I close my eyes tightly and pray that I'm having an out of body experience. Maybe I was exposed to something and it's causing hallucinations because by all accounts Evan Archer should not be sitting on *my* couch, in *my* house. The simplest answer to all of this is that he's an imposter and is infiltrating my family. My brother is dead, buried six feet under about fifteen miles from here. I know because I was just there talking to him.

I was here the day his body came off the plane. I identified him. I cried for him and for the loss my family was suffering. I held his fiancée in my arms so she wouldn't crumble to the ground from devastation at his funeral service. None of this makes sense, yet here sits a man who looks and speaks like my brother, only he can't be because my brother would *never* let me claim his son as my own.

I have two of Evan's most prized possessions and if the man before me actually is my brother, I just became public enemy number one.

EJ comes thundering down the stairs, shouting for me to come and join him. Evan's eyes are trained on him, and mine are on Evan. There's no handbook on how to handle this situation. Evan and I have never trained for anything like this.

It's unchartered territory, and I'm nervous. EJ passes by Ryley, who hasn't moved an inch since Evan sat down. I've noticed in the brief time they've been home that she watches him like a hawk. What I can't determine is if she's waiting for him to do something dangerous, or if she wants to crawl in his lap and tell him it's going to be okay. Never mind the fact that she still wears my ring on her finger, not his.

As soon as I sit down, EJ hops into my lap. He's blocking my view of Evan, and that gives me a little reprieve from the death glare.

"Nate, are you hungry?" Her voice is meek, unsure and sounding nothing like the Ryley she was when I left. I don't even want to know how many nights she's cried herself to sleep. In my mind, the only image I want to have of her sleeping while I was gone is by herself. But I know Evan well enough to know that he hasn't left her alone.

"I am, but I can make something."

She shakes her head. Her lower lip quivers as she pulls it into her mouth. EJ is restless on my lap and the tension in the air is so thick that it's suffocating. EJ taps me on the face, taking my attention away from Ryley.

"Did you hear'd me?"

Evan mutters something as he stands up and passes by, following Ryley into the kitchen. The eighteen year old in me wants to get up and go be the third wheel, much like I was in high school, but my son needs my attention.

"I'm sorry, buddy. Tell me again."

EJ prattles on about everything he's done while I've been gone, but I'm only picking up a few tidbits of information. Each time I hear "Eban" my train of thought diverts. I'm not being fair to my son right now and I hate that. Each and every time I've returned from deployment he has been given my utmost attention. He's curious about what I do and loves going to base with me. The guys love having him around too.

"Did you miss me?"

"Every day," I say with as much conviction as possible so he knows it's true. I'm not sure how long Evan's been home – if that's even Evan – and I don't want EJ thinking I'm being replaced because I'm not. I refuse to allow that to happen in his or Ryley's life.

"What did you do dis time?"

"Well let's see," I say as I pretend to ponder his question. The last time I was gone I told him I had to race around in a boat trying to rescue baby ducks that had missed their chance to fly south with their parents. He told me I was the coolest dad ever because I had saved all the babies so their mommies wouldn't be sad. In EJ's eyes, I'm a hero and I want to stay that way.

"This time a giant snake escaped from the zoo and I had to go help them find it."

He gasps and his little mouth drops open. I choke back a sob and paste on a smile just for him. My world is spinning right now and the more I think about what the next hour is going to bring, the faster it goes. My life is about to change and I'm not so confident I'm going to be the victor in any of this.

"Did you catch him?"

I nod more than a few times, hoping to find my voice. "Yeah we did," I say as my voice breaks at the end. I can't lose Ryley and EJ. They're my whole life. And my brother – my best friend – we should be celebrating the fact that he's home, but we're not because our lives are colossally screwed up.

"Nate?"

I look toward the familiar voice and smile. My sister, Olivia, is here, which can only mean one thing – she and Ryley are on speaking terms.

"Hey Liv, it's good to see you. I thought we'd have to take a trip up to Mom's to see you later in the week."

Livvie's face is pensive and her eyes are wandering around the room. She looks like she has something to say, but can't find the words and the longer she stands there, the more it dawns on me that she's here because of Evan. She didn't reconcile with Ryley while I was gone, it's because Evan came home.

"Did you go see Grandma, EJ?" I ask him because he's the only one who will give me an honest answer.

He nods. "Eban took us."

Of course he did, I think as I press my hand to my head so I can massage my temple. The headache that is coming on is going to be fierce and relentless. I'm single-handedly being pushed out of my family and there won't be a single thing I can do about it.

"Did you know?" she asks her voice barely above a whisper and breaking. I hate that she's about to cry.

I shake my head. My lips form into a thin line.

"How?"

I look at her questioningly. "How what, Olivia?"

Livvie sits down quietly and EJ leaves me to go sit with her. He'll never know how much my heart just broke in that moment, but I get it. He doesn't see her a lot. I live here with him... or at least I *think* I do. Hell, right now I'm not even sure I'm in any functioning reality.

"How could you not tell me that our brother was alive? How could you do this to Mom?"

"Yeah, Nate, how could you do this to Mom?"

Both of us turn to find Evan standing in the doorway looking as cocky as ever.

"You both are making assumptions that you shouldn't."

"You're twins! You have that freaky twin intuition. How could you not feel him or *something*?" Livvie pleads with me. I wish I had the answer she was looking for, but I don't.

"Tink, why don't you take EJ upstairs?" Evan says, asserting his control over the situation. "We need to have a conversation that EJ probably shouldn't hear."

"Can I take him for ice cream?"

"No," I say.

"Yes," Evan says at the same time. Liv looks back and forth between the two of us and Evan nods. I'm going to concede this one, but this will be it. I'm EJ's dad, not him, and Ryley's *my* fiancée. If Evan thinks that we're just going to go back to the way things were, he's out of his mind... if he's even who he says he is. For all we know, he's an imposter. He's someone who has stolen my brother's identity and is about to steal my life.

EJ hops down from her lap and pulls her hand into his. They're out the front door before I can even tell him goodbye.

"How are you Evan?" I ask before he has a chance to say anything. By the way he's standing I know he's looking for a fight. He smirks and shakes his head.

"I should be asking you the same thing. How did it feel to be me for a while?"

I run my fingers through my hair, which is in serious need of a shave. Being gone for a month with no amenities takes its toll and I prefer to keep my hair as short as I can.

"I'm not sure what you're referring to, but if it's Ryley

and EJ, I'm here because this is where you wanted me to be." I stand and start pacing. There's no way I'm going to let him attack me because of this. "You died, Evan. I identified your body. How you are standing here makes no sense. It's unnatural."

"I'm here because I *didn't* die. You *didn't* identify me. You identified someone else." He pushes himself off the wall and comes toward me just as Ryley steps into view with my sandwich in her hand. "The way I see it, little brother, you couldn't wait to get Ryley all to yourself and EJ was an added bonus. You get to play Daddy in *my* house with *my* girl and *my* son while I'm out in the damn jungle thinking about them every fucking day.

"So how was it, Nate? Did you conveniently ignore radio comms? Did you just happen to forget where I was? I'm hoping you can enlighten me because this is seriously fucked up and as far as I'm concerned, you're the one who's dead. You're dead to me."

Evan is standing nose to nose with me. I can feel the inhale and exhale of his chest against mine. He's the only man that I can do this with. He's the only man that can break me without even trying. But I'm not going to let that happen. We're about to battle, and it's not over some foreign land, a corrupt leader or political views. It's over two people that we love the most in the world, the only two people who could destroy the both of us in a single solitary second.

His words echo through my mind... *I'm dead to him.* He doesn't mean that. I know deep down that he's angry, hurt and probably confused. I would be too. I know better than to take what he's saying to heart, regardless of how much it hurts. He's my brother. We're bound by blood.

42

Small hands separate us, causing us both to step back. Evan's anger is seeping through him and if I wasn't the one on the other end of his torment, I'd tell whoever was to run. I'm not running.

"I didn't know," is all I can say as Ryley pushes me toward the steps and out of the living room.

chapter 8
Evan

TIME MOVES IN SLOW MOTION as Ryley pushes Nate up the stairs, the stairs that lead to the bedrooms, bedrooms that I don't want her and Nate anywhere near. I've always been possessive of Ryley, even in high school. Once we started dating, guys flirted with her like crazy. Sometimes, her naiveté played in my favor because she didn't realize they were doing it, or at least she didn't let on that she'd noticed. Either way, I hated it. It drove me nuts that other guys thought that they had a chance with her, but on the other hand it was the biggest ego boost that she didn't care.

The possessiveness started a few months before graduation. There was a guy in particular who was in her grade who couldn't seem to grasp that she was with me. His name was Butler. John, Jeff, something with a J, I believe. We played football together, but other than that we weren't friends. When he found out I had enlisted, he told Ry that he would be her shoulder to cry on. I wanted to set him straight, but Nate told me not to do anything to mess up my enlistment. A few days later, Butler showed up to school with a broken collarbone. I never asked Nate if he was responsible, but always suspected it. I never thanked him either because I didn't want to acknowledge that he got to do what I wanted to do.

After that I made sure it was clear that she and I were together and short of pissing on her leg like a damn fire hydrant, all the guys in school knew she was taken. I let them all believe that I was the one who messed up Butler, and he never told them otherwise. When I would come home, I made sure to show up at school to surprise my girl, even in college.

Now, watching her with my brother makes me feel like an outsider. They share something that I may never understand. They were close before, but never like this. Now, seeing my girl clutch his t-shirt causes enough physical pain that my insides hurt. They share a connection that I'm not a part of.

I can't lose her. Not having Ryley in my life is not something I've ever planned for. Knowing at eighteen that you've met the one person you were destined to be with is life changing. When she lay on the ground after I hit her, I knew. I knew she was the one and I wasn't afraid to admit it. Never did I think that I'd be better with anyone else because she was the best of me. She made me want to be the best for her.

They talk too quietly for me to hear. I'm standing in the middle of a living room that I barely remember while they stand together on the stairs, and I can't hear a single word they're saying. And I can't help but feel lost, left out and like I don't belong. I step closer, only for Nate to turn and stomp up the stairs. Ryley makes eye contact with me. She descends slowly, never breaking our connection.

"What's going on?"

Her hands brush over my shoulder, just like the many times she'd straighten out my uniform or my NWU's. As her hands trail down my arms and into my hands, her fingers lock with mine.

"I need you to do me a favor."

I sigh and squeeze her hands with mine. "If this were any other situation I'd say anything, but I'm almost afraid of what you might ask of me."

Ryley's eyes meet mine, they're wet and I know I'm the cause of her tears. She tries to smile but her lips form a thin line, making me wonder what the hell has just happened. We were fine at the beach and everything was fine in the kitchen. What happened in the few short minutes with Nate that would make everything change?

"I need to talk to Nate and I can't do that with you here. You're angry with him and I get that, but as much as this hurts, Nate lives here. And right now I'm on the edge, about to fall off the damn cliff of confusion and need both of you to meet me half way."

"You want me to leave you here with him?" I let go of one of her hands and point up to the ceiling, the general direction to where Nate is currently hiding out like a coward.

"He's not going to hurt me."

I scoff. "Right, because he loves you."

Ryley nods and I feel defeated. "You're choosing him?"

"No, I'm choosing me. I'm choosing EJ. I'm asking that you give me time to talk to Nate. Time to figure things out so I know what the hell is going on with my life. He says he didn't know, Evan, that has to mean something to you –"

"It means nothing."

"Don't interrupt me. I've earned the right to speak my mind," she scolds, taking a deep breath. "For the past month I have questioned everything I've known since the last time I saw you walk out the door. I've even questioned what I know about Nate, and that's not fair to him."

Ryley places her hands on my cheeks, keeping my eyes focused on her. "I love you, Archer. And if you love me, you'll give me what I'm asking. I need to talk to Nate without your interference. He has that right, just as I gave it to you."

I nod, knowing she's right. Leaning forward, I place a kiss on her forehead and hold my lips there as long as I can. When I pull away I hear her sniffle. I hate that she's crying. I don't want to cause her tears, but my fear is if I give her what she's asking for, I'm going to lose.

"I'll be at River's," I say as I walk away.

I choose to sit on the steps of River's house instead of knocking. I shouldn't have come here, but he was the obvious choice. Three of us returned to find different lives and each of us have to find a way to deal with what's happened. Tucker McCoy can't find his wife and daughter. Justin Rask's parents want nothing to do with him. Then there's my situation with Ryley and Nate. River, whose wife welcomed him home with open arms as if nothing happened, is the only one who isn't submerged in drama.

Coming here was wrong. He's not going to understand. As far as he's concerned everything is perfect. His wife was waiting for him, holding vigil until he returned. She, unlike the rest of our families, held out hope her husband was alive. Why her and not Ryley? If anything, I would've expected Ryley to question everything. Maybe she did, but didn't get anywhere. She wasn't my wife so her hands were tied. Fact of the matter is that if she's not legally a spouse, she has no rights as far as the military is concerned.

The door opens before I can make my decision to leave. The heavy footfalls tell me it's River. He sits down next to me and hands me a beer. I've been out in the sun all day; I'm over-emotional and tired and a beer is the last thing I need, but it feels damn good going down the back of my throat.

"Want to talk about it?"

I shake my head and take another drink from the bottle, downing most of it. My fingers glide over the imprinted label. No longer paper, but melted into the glass.

"When did they change the bottles?"

He shrugs. He doesn't know any more than I do. We've lost six years and the people who were tasked with protecting us did such a stand up job that they forgot to tell us we're all dead or, at the very least, fill us in on everything we missed - like beer bottles with no paper labels. I suppose the bogus letters we received from home should've been enough to keep us in the loop but they weren't.

"Nate's back and she asked me to leave so she could talk to him."

River is silent next to me. Only the birds, traffic and planes flying overhead curb the dullness between us. When I'm with Ryley, I can open up. I can tell her how I'm feeling or what I'm thinking. But sitting here with River, opening up is the last thing I want to do. He's not going to understand because he *has* his wife. He came home to everything that he left behind and the only thing he lost was time.

"You knew he was bound to return."

"Deep down I was hoping he'd be gone for six years so I could undo everything that's been done." I tap my beer bottle against the brick step, listening to the clank it makes with each hit. "They have a connection. It's there; I saw it. He loves her, he always has, and I'm afraid I may be too late. I'm not sure if what we have… *had*… will be enough to break through what they share."

"Your death brought them together?"

I nod. "Yep, as much as I don't want to admit it, they bonded over someone they lost, then EJ arrived and he was the link that kept them together. I think that if EJ hadn't been born, Nate wouldn't have hung around, but he was doing what I asked of him… he was taking care of my family. He just took it a step too far."

Once again, only the outdoor noises keep the awkward silences at bay. We're just two guys sitting on a stoop. From an outsider's point of view, we're just hanging out. Only he knows that I've been asked to leave my girl alone with the one man who stands between us.

As I sit here with him I can't help but want to ask him something that's been plaguing my mind since we came back. I hesitate, though, because if I ask him what I'm thinking it could put a serious dent in our relationship and I don't want that to happen. I've already lost enough.

I breathe in and exhale loudly in frustration causing him to look at me. "What's up?" he asks with a knowing expression on his face.

Scratching the back of my head, I realize it's now or never.

I look over my shoulder at his house before looking at him. "Have you asked yourself why Frannie was waiting for you? I mean, look at us — we were dead to them. Rask's parents won't talk to him. McCoy's wife and daughter are long gone. Ryley's moved on. You're the only one who came home to everything as normal as it was when we left."

River's forehead wrinkles, but he doesn't try to strangle me so I count this as a win in my book. He looks over his shoulder, staring at his house before turning back and setting his bottle down.

"I've asked myself that every day. I've tried to talk to Frannie about it, asking her why she didn't move on, and all she says is that she couldn't. She just knew I was alive."

Those are words I'd love to hear from Ryley, and even Nate. Knowing that one of them thought I was alive and that they never gave up on me would be worth this bullshit I'm dealing with now.

chapter 9
Nate

LIFE IS UNPREDICTABLE. LIFE IS messy. Life throws you curve balls when you're expecting a slider. My brother is back from the dead... or undead, not dead, however it needs to be spun. The simple truth is that he's alive. No, there's nothing simple about the truth because we don't actually know what that truth is. How can someone you buried years ago suddenly be alive? Not just him either, but a four man crew. Each and every one of them gone, with families that have moved on, only to find their loved one is, in fact, alive and well.

For a brief moment I thought that Evan was a prisoner of war, but that's not the case. He's been fed, taken care of, and even groomed – POW's don't have those liberties. There would've been a ransom or some kind of demand. *I* would've hunted for him until I brought him home. *I* would've gone to the ends of earth and back until he was safe with me.

Evan and I need to talk.

Brother to brother.

Warrior to warrior.

Whether he wants to or not.

This cloud of Ryley and EJ looming over us is a different matter. He will never be able to think clearly, to see us as brothers, as long as I'm with Ryley. Leaving her isn't an option, though. I love her, and I know she loves me. It's not as straightforward as just packing up and leaving. We're a family. When I'm home we have routines from grocery shopping, to eating out once a week. Evan wants his family, and I want to keep mine. It's not going to matter what decision is made, someone is going to get hurt.

As soon as the door shuts, I walk back downstairs. When Ryley asked if she could speak to Evan alone, I couldn't say no. He's been back for a month and I'm already imagining the worst happening. I don't want to think that she cheated, but the thoughts are there. Any man in my position would think the same. I hate that I am, but my gut is telling me she cheated.

Standing in the doorway to the kitchen, Ryley fiddles with the few dishes in the sink. My uneaten sandwich sits on the table, wrapped in plastic wrap and waiting for me to devour it. My stomach growls, but I can't eat. The thought of food right now makes my stomach twist into knots. My relationship with Ryley is about to be tested and it's very unsettling.

The urge to go to her, to stand behind her and kiss her neck is as strong as it was before I left. I'm not sure how I'm supposed to act right now. Are we still engaged or did she call that off the minute Evan showed up? Yesterday, I was talking about getting married and hopefully conceiving another child before I deployed, but now I'm not even certain that she wants me to touch her. I've always been second to Evan in her eyes;

that's something I've accepted. He's her first true love and nothing ever replaces that.

My steps are cautious and yet calculated as I approach her. She sees me out of the corner of her eye but continues to wash the dishes. I reach around, shutting off the water and encasing her with my arms. I hold her as she sags against me. The first sob breaks my heart and the second shatters it to pieces. Her knees buckle and I guide us to the floor, bringing her onto my lap. Her tears soak my shirt, intensifying the ache I'm already feeling for her.

We've been here before, on the kitchen floor with her on my lap. After I was given the news about Evan, I left the base in Afghanistan and came straight to her. Something told me that she'd need me more than my mother would and I was right. Ryley wasn't just alone after losing Evan, but pregnant as well. No one knew at the time, except for her and Evan... and then me. Ryley hadn't gotten around to telling anyone in hopes that Evan wouldn't be gone long. This time it's different but with the same result, heartbreaking tears over my brother.

Holding her against my chest, my hand rubs up and down her back in an attempt to soothe her. It makes me wonder if she did this with Evan – or even Lois – or if she's been holding on until I got home. This is a side of Ryley that Evan has never seen. He wasn't there to pick her up off the bathroom floor after she spent all night crying in there. He wasn't around to make sure she ate, or went to her doctor's appointments. He wasn't pacing the floor, desperate to get into the delivery room with each cry he heard.

That was me.

He would've been there for all of those things, given the chance. My brother would *not* have missed the birth of his son;

I know that for a fact. I also know he never did anything to make Ryley cry, nothing intentional at least, and would've been the first one to scoop her up in his arms and fix whatever was causing her pain.

I couldn't do that for her then, and I can't do that for her now. He's the cause. It'd be easy for me to remind her that these tears are all because of him, but I can't. He's my brother and whether he sees us that way or not, I refuse to badmouth him.

Ryley turns in my arms, her head resting on my shoulder. "He just showed up. I came home from the store, and he was here. He looked the same, he spoke the same, but… remember when I thought I'd see Evan at the beach or coming off base? You'd remind me that he wasn't coming back, and yet there he was in the flesh. I screamed at him, Nate. I said mean, hurtful things to him when he hadn't done anything wrong.

"He just stood there, dumbfounded and hurt. That hurt quickly turned to anger when he saw my ring and I told him who it was from. The look in his eyes, it's something I've never seen from him. And then when he asked about EJ, I lost it."

"What do you mean when he asked about EJ?" I ask, in confusion. Evan knew she was pregnant, but he couldn't have known his son's name.

"That's just it, he knew. He knew *everything*. Evan had pictures of EJ and me. He had letters from us. Packages from home… None of them died. Him, River, McCoy and Rask were all getting care packages and letters."

Ryley's words stun me and as much as I'd like to call bullshit, I know she's telling the truth. Words rattle around in my brain, but nothing comes out of my mouth. Who would do this to us? To the team? And why?

"Did Evan say where he was?"

Ryley shakes her head. I knew that'd be her answer that he wouldn't divulge classified information, but I had to ask. Instead of leaning against me, where I'd like her to be, she sits up. Her beautiful face is stained from tears, her gorgeous red hair is falling out of her ponytail and her eyes are puffy and red. It's been years since I've seen her like this. We've been happy for so long and for this to happen, while it should be a miracle, is unheard of.

"I love him," she says, her voice breaking. I knew this was coming I was just hoping that it wouldn't be today or tomorrow. Can I live with her knowing that she's in love with Evan? Yes, I know I can because I have been for years... but he wasn't here then. He is now.

"I know you do."

"I don't know what to do."

My eyes close for fear that I'm going to break down in front of her. She's only seen me cry a few times and right now doesn't need to be another. I know what's coming. I knew the minute I saw them walk in together.

"Ry, I can't tell you what to do. Hell, I don't even know what the answer is. Our lives have been rocked by tragedy and we've survived so I'm pretty sure we can survive this. Whether it be together or apart, we do it together. But before you make a decision, know how much I love you. Know how much I love EJ."

I take a deep breath and pull her back into my arms. It may be the last time I get to hold her, although I plan to do everything in my power to ensure that's not the case. "You and EJ, you're my world. I don't want to lose you. I *can't* lose you. You make me tick. You're my better half. You give me something to look forward to at the end of the night. You've been my rock for as long as I can remember. We're about to get married and expand our family... none of that has to change. I've known for years that you love Evan, and I've respected that."

"It's different, Nate."

I know that, but I don't tell her. I hold her because for all I know she's going to tell me to pack my shit and leave. That's not what I want and it's not what she needs. Being alone with her thoughts is a dangerous thing for her.

"Someone did this to us, Nate. Why would they do this?"

"I don't know but I promise you I'm going to find out."

It's in this moment that I vow to find out how this happened. I don't know how, but I'm going to. Someone has to pay for what they've done to my family. Someone has to answer for what they've put Ryley through. Imagining the agony of seeing Evan alive after everything she went through; I can't even begin to describe how angry it makes me knowing I wasn't home to help her. Losing my brother was unthinkable, but I have never seen someone break the way she has. When my father died, my mother cried but was stoic. Ryley crumbled. She lost her world and wanted to crawl into a hole and never come out, but she couldn't. Being pregnant saved her life as far as I'm concerned.

"I don't want Livvie here," I blurt out, losing my filter. My sister hasn't been Ryley's cheerleader these past few years and the fact that she's here is rubbing me the wrong way.

"She's your sister," Ryley says so quietly that had there been any noise, I wouldn't have heard her. I pull her a little closer and kiss the top of her head, leaving my nose and mouth pressed there.

"I know," I say after pulling away. "But her intentions aren't to help you with EJ, she's here because she wants to be with Evan. If that's what she wants, she can go stay at Carter's."

I know my timing probably sucks but I want to lay down some ground rules about Livvie being here. I don't like it and don't believe that Livvie is here for anyone but Evan. I know she won't do anything to hurt EJ, but that doesn't mean she won't be a brat to Ryley as she always has been.

"Your mom kicked her out."

Sighing, my head taps lightly against the cabinet. When Evan died, my mother shut off. I thought when she found out about EJ things would change, but sometimes I think his birth just made things worse for her. Livvie was always closer to Evan than she was to me, which never bothered me until she all but alienated Ryley. Most of that was due to my mother, and the fact that Ryley and I started dating.

"My mom..." I cut myself off before I can even begin to defend her.

"Thinks I'm a whore."

Her words sting because Ryley is anything but. I turn slightly so I can look into her eyes. "You're not a whore. Why would you even say that?"

Her eyes fill up with tears again and my heart plummets, expecting the words "I cheated" to come out of her mouth even though I don't want to believe she could do that to me. I know how Evan feels about her, though, and if he didn't know she'd thought he was dead, he'd have expected her to wait for him.

"I kissed him, Nate. I did it more than once and I wanted more. I'm sorry, but I did it and I hate myself."

Kissing I can live with even though I shouldn't have to.

Sex is another story. Regardless of where Evan has been, we knew him as dead. After we buried him we all worked to move on and provide for EJ. None of it was easy.

"Ry –"

"No, please listen. When I see him, I'm taken back to what we had and what we've missed out on. It's hard to not want to be with him, but it's also hard not to want to be with you as well. I'm confused, hurt, and angry and I feel incredibly lost right now. I'm a nightmare when all I wanted to be was a fairytale.

"Life isn't a fairytale, Ry." I cup her cheek and she covers my hand with hers. Her smile is soft and hits me right in my heart.

"My life has felt like a fairytale, for the most part, since I met you and Evan. You both have made me feel like I'm a princess in your own ways."

I pull her close and press my lips to hers. The soft feel of her lips give me hope. Even though she's in my arms, I feel distant, like this is an out of body experience. Hell, maybe I'm hallucinating. I'm still in the desert waiting to shoot my rifle and when I come home she's waiting for me with open arms and none of this is happening. But just as I told her that life isn't a fairytale, it's not a dream either.

It's reality, and reality is ugly.

"Everything's going to be okay," I say, pulling her into my arms. When she sags against me I know deep down that she and I are going to be together. I don't know how but we'll make it work, taking a vow that we have planned to stay with each other, for better or for worse, and apply it now. Ryley has to know that I'm in this for the long haul no matter what.

Before I can reassure her that I'm not going anywhere the

front door opens, but Ryley doesn't move. Knowing that it could be Evan and she's still in my arms comforts me. It's hard not to think about what lies ahead. The road before us isn't forking, it's damn well splitting with too many options. Sadly, not a single option is favorable for all parties involved. Life is going to get messy, and I hate messy. I need order.

High pitched squeals and the thundering of little feet brings a smile to my face. I've missed my boy, and hate that I have to leave him again, but my duty is to my country. I know that each time I'm gone I'm protecting his future.

EJ comes around the corner, his smile spreading from ear to ear as he barrels toward us. Ryley catches him and maneuvers him between us. I have my family. We may be slightly unconventional, but we work. We love each other. Livvie clears her throat, making eye contact with me. I don't even have to ask what she's thinking; I can see displeasure written all over her face. The brother part of me should get up and talk to her, but holding my family in my arms is far more important.

I don't know how long we sit on the kitchen floor holding each other, an hour maybe two. I'm not counting. I'd love to find a way to keep us here and shut out the outside world forever or for us to run off into the sunset and forget everyone around us. But truth be told, life just isn't that easy - it's unorganized, dysfunctional and crazy.

Take it from me... if you think your life is perfect, you're lying to yourself.

chapter 10
Evan

THE SMELL OF BARBECUED FOOD wafts through the air. As I look around River's neighborhood I remember that most of the homes belong to sailors and their families. Before we left, there was a block party. We all came together, ate, drank and had a blast. Music played, people got to know each other and everyone had a good time. Everyone laughed. I remember thinking that I couldn't wait to have one on my block, but that never happened. And sitting here now, watching the kids ride their bikes up and down the street, I'm not sure it'll ever happen.

"I want this," I say, spreading my arms out wide. "I want to see EJ riding his bike with his friends. I want bikes parked in my front yard and noise coming from my house. I want people to know that they can stop by anytime, just to say hi. That's how my house was when Nate and I were growing up. My mom would bake cookies at night for the next day and my friends would be over all the time. It all stopped when we were sophomores and discovered that making out was better than Mom's cookies."

"You'll have it," River says, but his voice lacks the conviction I need to believe him. It's hard for me to grasp that I can have what I want. I had it, but the Navy took it away.

"I don't even know if I have a place to live," I reply as I shake my head in frustration. "She asked me to leave, but never said to go back in an hour or two. She just asked, and I did it without hesitation because I'd do anything for her." My pity party of one is growing by leaps and bounds. I shouldn't be here dumping this on him; he has his own issues to work out. But I have nowhere else to go, at least no place that I trust.

"Ryley's going through a lot, but I doubt she'll kick you out."

I scoff. "I'm not living with my brother. So either he leaves or I do and something tells me that it's going to be me. He can claim squatter's rights or whatever they're called and there isn't jack shit I can do about it. Nate's lived there for the past however many years. He's taken care of the house, EJ and as much as I hate admitting it, Ryley. I'm Charlie Bucket from *Willy Wonka*, looking through the window at the candy counter."

Tipping the bottle back, I empty what's left of its contents. Dwelling on what I can't fix isn't going to make things better for me and it's definitely not going to improve my situation with Ryley. However, leaving her with my brother doesn't sit well with me. I'll have to fight to keep her and EJ, and he's my enemy. I need to be front and present. I can't be forgotten again.

"You know you can stay here," River assures me. I know I can, but imposing is not in my nature, especially to a couple who could be going through the same things Ryley and I are. Six years is a long time to go without seeing each other, and to find each other again takes time. Time is not my friend right now.

"You and Frannie need time. I don't want to impose."

River looks over his shoulder quickly and shakes his head. "I'm home, but things are different. She doesn't ask questions and acts like nothing is amiss. My clothes were still hanging in my closet, my boots by the door. My favorite beer was in the refrigerator and when I went to throw it out she said she had just bought it. I'm not sure what to think. Either she really held out hope, or she's not right in the head."

I try not laugh, but can't keep it in. "That's your wife you're talking about."

He shakes his head. "I know, and I'm trying to tell myself that she was just keeping everything because she hoped I would return, but it's just odd especially when she buried me. Either way, you're welcome here until… well, as long as you need. I could use the company."

"Thanks, man."

A couple of River's neighbors walk by, stopping to chat, and a few venture into territory that neither of us are willing to talk about. Everyone wants to know what happened. Where we've been and how we're doing. Each neighbor is caring, offering us their shoulder as if we'd divulge our lives to them. That's what I have Doc Howard for. I've told her classified information, facts that could possibly get me dishonorably discharged, but I trust her. Telling a stranger walking down the street, however, is never gonna happen.

"They're nosey, yet caring."

River chuckles. "You have no idea. The first night I was

home, the doorbell rang every thirty seconds and every visitor brought food. Frannie doesn't know this, but I took most of it down to the shelter."

"Very noble of you."

"Nah," he says as he pops open another beer. "Do you ever wonder why the press isn't hounding us? We were dead, Archer, and then showed up out of the blue as if nothing happened. Where are the talk shows and book deals?"

What he's saying makes me wonder about the same thing and it perplexes me. We should be all over national TV and signing deals right and left to tell our story.

"Everything about that mission is a mystery. We extracted the package, only to be sent out continuously. We should've been home within ten days. Someone wanted us gone and we have to find out why and who." Thinking about what I want to say next and making it sound plausible and not some lame ass attempt on my part to get Nate out of the way, is tricky. Sighing, I run my hand through my hair and stand.

"I know this woman. She works for Navy Intelligence – at least she did before we left. I'm going to call her up and see if she can help. Hopefully with her and Carole we can learn something. We've been home a month and I have a feeling shit isn't even stirring enough to hit the fan."

"Who is she?"

Smirking, I think this name will get a rise out of River. "Cara Hughes," I pause to see if he has any recollection of who she is. When he doesn't, I continue. "She was Nate's girlfriend when we left."

River's eyes meet mine and disappointment is written all over his face. His head moves back and forth slowly. I know he's not going to approve, but Cara is a viable option for help.

She'll be able to gain access to confidential and hidden files, which is what I'm assuming is needed.

"You're playing a dangerous game, Archer."

"I know, but with her connections —"

"To Nate?"

"No, not necessarily," I say with a shake of my head. "Cara can access files that Carole can't. She's trained to find answers."

"She's Nate's ex. Don't tell me you're bringing her around to see if she can get him away from Ryley?"

The thought of using Cara like that hadn't crossed my mind. From what I remember, they were in love but I don't even know if she's still around.

"It's not that, River. Clearly something happened between them since he's engaged to Ryley, but I'm hoping she can help. Honestly, I don't even know where to find her, it'll be a shot in the dark."

River nods and looks like he's contemplating what I'm saying. I could be grasping at straws where Cara is concerned. I don't know why she and my brother are no longer together. It could be a number of things, one being Ryley got in the way.

"Like I said, it's a long shot, but it's better than not doing anything." I sigh, exasperated. I want the answers to all my questions put down on a piece of paper and handed to me on a silver platter.

"I'm going to get going," I say, needing to clear my head.

"Where?"

I shrug. "I don't know, for a drive. I just need to think."

"What should I tell Ryley when she calls?"

Looking up and down the road I'd love to think that Ryley is at home wondering where I am, but I have a feeling she's not. My return interrupted her life and now that Nate's home, her life is probably going back to normal.

"She won't," I say as I step off the curb and head to my car. It's a stab to my heart thinking the way I do, but the alternative isn't much better. For all I know, they're happy and plan to get married whether I approve or not.

Walking into Magoo's feels like old times. I've only visited my favorite establishment once since I've been back and I hadn't realized how much I missed hanging out here. We'd stop here at least once or twice a week after work, just to be normal. This is where McCoy met his wife. She was here looking for trouble and found it in the name of Tucker McCoy. Many consider Magoo's a meat market. Women flock here in hopes of picking up a SEAL or higher-ranking sailor.

The walls are covered with photos of military members who have long since left us. Our images were up, but as I look around I see a new memorial for them. The four of us hang together with a flag draped around us and in chicken scratch writing, the note says: *Home and Never Forgotten*. If I weren't so fond of the owner and bartender, Slick Rick, I'd tell him to take this shit down.

We may be home, but we were definitely forgotten.

Taking a seat at the bar, a frosty mug with some amber liquid is placed before me. Rick is only the third owner of this bar, a bar that has held a lot of homecomings for sailors and a few Marines. He took over from his grandfather when he was barely able to drink himself. This place is old and in need of some major renovations, but that's what gives it character. In the corner is an old jukebox that plays songs from the seventies and eighties, and is the only thing that provides us music.

"You seem to be missing your crew." Rick wipes down the section of bar I'm sitting at and sets down a fresh bowl of nuts. I pick a few up, tossing them in my mouth. If Ryley were here, she'd frown and remind me that the other guy who put his hands in there probably didn't wash them after using the restroom. Right now, my response would be: If I could survive in the jungle for six years, nothing is going to kill me.

"We're all trying to find a way to deal."

"Makes sense."

I glance at Rick, who busies himself with restocking glasses. He's lingering near me, maybe wanting to talk. The thought never occurred to me that he hears things working here. He may have information on what happened with my crew.

"Things been good?" I ask, breaking the stillness. Rick looks around, his head moving from side to side. I try to follow his gaze, looking at the patrons in the bar, but don't recognize anyone. More often than not, people come and go. Duties change, deployments happen, or you get transferred to another base. Being a SEAL, my base options are limited. It's one of the things I love about my job.

"Business is always good, better now that you guys are back."

"Oh yeah, why's that?" His words pique my curiosity.

Rick sets his hands on the bar and leans in. "People are asking a lot of questions. There's been a news reporter hanging around. She comes in every other night or so, lurking.

You know how I feel about reporters, but she keeps to herself. She's waiting for one of you to come in is what I'm guessing."

This is exactly what River and I were discussing earlier. Where is all the media hoopla with us returning? Four men do not return from the dead, alive and well, without the media circus. Where's the hero's welcome? The parade? The banners? Why aren't the television crews camped outside our houses waiting to tell our stories?

"She here now?"

Rick shakes his head subtly alerting me that someone is here that he's not too fond of. I look around, but don't see anyone I recognize, which isn't saying much since I've only seen a few faces since my miraculous return home.

"Who has you bothered, Rick?"

He nods, and I look over my shoulder. "That's Senator Lawson."

"Never heard of him," I say, turning my gaze back to Rick.

"You wouldn't. He's not from here. He's a representative of Florida. The first time I saw him was about a month or two before you guys left. He was in the corner with O'Keefe. I hadn't seen him again until you guys came home."

My mouth feels like its dropping open and my eyes are bugging out, much like you'd see on Saturday morning cartoons. I don't care if there's a connection or not, what Rick just said seems very out of the ordinary. Why would this guy suddenly be back in Magoo's now that we've returned?

Rick leaves to tend to other patrons and clean a few tables. I keep my eyes focused on my beer and occasionally glance in the mirror to watch the Senator. I need to tell River and the guys, see what they know or how we can investigate who this guy is and what his relationship is with our Captain. O'Keefe walked off our plane into a waiting car and we haven't heard from him in a month. This reeks of a cover up, but I need to know why and what exactly we were involved with.

A soft, warm hand brings me out my bubble. To my side stands my girl. Her long red hair is pulled up on top of her head in a messy bun. The shorts and tank top she had on earlier have been replaced with yoga pants and a sweatshirt. Her beautiful angelic face is free of any make-up. She smiles at me, and just like that I know that whatever she has to say, I'm going to listen.

Everything in me is telling me to pull her into my arms and hold her, never letting go, but that's not why she's here. She's chosen Nate and as much as it's going to hurt, he's the safest choice for her.

chapter 11
Nate

EJ TALKS ABOUT EVAN THE entire way to Carter's. It feels good to hear about my brother bonding with his son, but at what expense. Mine? Ryley's? How is EJ going to feel or even understand that Evan is his father and I'm not? That isn't something I'm willing to tell him, at least not at the age of five. He's not going to comprehend that what his mother and I did was for his own benefit. How do you explain that we were only trying to give him the family that he deserved? You don't.

As soon as we're parked, he's out of the car and running toward the door. Grace, Carter and Lois's daughter, is his best friend. Lois and Ryley joke that they'll get married someday, much to the loud groans of Carter. I don't really have a take on the whole situation. I'm a guy with a son. It's not in my genes to worry about who he dates. I'll leave that up to Ryley.

Lois meets us at the door and takes our bags from me. She kisses my cheek before allowing me to step inside. I take her in, her brunette hair and small five-foot-two frame.

"Carter's out back," she says with a smile. Just the sound of his name makes her dark eyes sparkle.

"Thanks," I say as I give her another kiss on the cheek before walking through the house toward the back door. Grace and EJ are already upstairs, making a racket. Their laughter echoes through the house and their footfalls shake the walls. I wish I could be a kid again, to be able to laugh and play without any worries. What I wouldn't give to go back to those carefree days.

As soon as the door shuts behind me, the noise level drops. No wonder Carter has chosen to have his man cave in the backyard. A few years ago he called me over to help him build a shed but what he ended up with is far from a shed - it's big enough to hold a couch and two recliners, a large screen TV and a "beererator".

Rapping my knuckles against the door, I turn the knob and step in before Carter has a chance to get up from his chair. Not that he really would, everyone is welcome. My best friend since high school is relaxed, lying back with his feet propped up and a beer resting in his hand.

"Sup," he says, as if he knows nothing of what's been going on. Carter is the type of guy who will wait for me to tell him what's on my mind before he starts offering advice. Mostly, he'll just listen. He and Lois have been together since high school, but haven't married yet. It's not because they don't love each other, but more so because they wanted other things first, like this house or their cars. I was hoping that when I came over today, it would be so I could ask him to stand up for me at my own wedding, not for a place to stay.

"Did you know?"

Carter shuts the television off and sits up in his chair, setting his bottle down on the table beside him. "Ryley called Lois. I could hear her screaming through the phone; I thought she had been hurt. I was putting on my shoes, about to go over there and kill someone, but Lois just shook her head. She had tears streaming down her face and I thought 'my god we've lost Nate'.

"I was pulling at Lois, much like Grace does when she wants attention and Lois kept slapping my hand away. When she mouthed 'Evan' my blood turned cold. I didn't wait to hear anything else. I left and went over to your house, but he was already gone."

Carter stands up and starts to pace. When he looks at me, I see anguish. He walks over to the wall and pulls down a picture of Evan, Carter and me from high school. The three of us played football together, and it was Carter who introduced Lois to Ryley. It was either by happenstance or fate that those two became best friends. After Carter and Lois graduated from college, they both looked for jobs in San Diego so we'd all be close. It's always meant a lot to us that they chose to be close to their friends, leaving their families behind.

"I haven't seen him," he continues. "I stay at home when Lois goes over there because I don't know how I'll react. I mean, what if it's not Evan? What will I do if I see him touch her? What if he hurts her and EJ?"

Carter puts the framed photo back, making sure it's straight before he sits down again. I'm not sure Evan will ever know how much his death affected everyone, not just Ryley.

Sighing, I pull at the ends of my hair. "I've thought the same thing, about it not being Evan. He's changed... he's angry. But I think that's to be expected. Ryley believes it's him and I know that's what she wants, but I'm still skeptical."

"Are you going to order a DNA test?"

I shrug. "I could, but we'd probably have to go someplace where no one knows us. If he *is* Evan, then something is up. I did a DNA test when his body was flown back. I had to make sure. So if that test came back positive, and my brother was in fact alive, what's this next test going to prove? You don't go on a mission for six years. You don't get buried for years. And you certainly don't show up again as if nothing has happened."

"He's not the only one, right?" Carter asks. I nod in agreement, but I don't really know much about the other members of the Team.

"Did he say where he was?"

Shaking my head, Carter knows I'm not going to answer. He may be my best friend, but he knows his boundaries. He respects my job and my inability to tell him about what I do.

"I'm sure Lois told you what's going on," I say vaguely, unable to speak the words it would take to actually explain any further. "Ryley wants space. She said she needs time to figure out her feelings and the future. It sucks and I have no choice but to accept it, but it's still hard to understand. We've been living together for a while and now I just feel lost."

"What about Evan?"

I groan and lean back. "She left to tell him before I came over here. I asked her if I could take EJ since I just got home. Ry promised me that she's telling him the same thing."

"Do you believe her?"

"Yeah, call me a stupid man in love but I do. I don't think she'd lie to me. Especially not after being lied to about Evan being dead."

"How are you doing with all of this? I mean with your

brother being back?" Carter isn't one to delve into feelings, call it the macho man in him and what not, but he avoids the touchy feely stuff like the plague. It makes me wonder if Lois gave him a speech about making sure I'm okay before I arrived.

"I'm confused, man. I buried him. I mourned. Part of me died when he did and now that he's back – a homecoming like this should be celebrated – but I can't wrap my head around it. We moved on and now my life is a soap opera without the cheesy music playing in the background. I should be planning my wedding, having a bachelor party and taking my wife on a honeymoon.

"I'm angry that Ryley has been put in this situation, that someone had the gall to fuck with my family, and for what? That's what I want to know, where the hell have these guys been and why? Why tell us they're dead and then bring them home? What did we do to deserve this?"

"It's been crazy for all of you, from what Lois has said. People don't believe what they're being told."

"Everything is so fucked."

Carter must agree because he nods. He stands, and I follow. It's late and the kids need to go to bed. EJ will want to stay in Grace's room, and I'd usually be okay with that, but tonight I want him with me. I know I'll have no choice but to share him with both Evan and Ryley after tonight so right now, I can't help but be selfish.

When we get back in the house, Lois is curled up on the couch with a book in her hands. She smiles at Carter, who kisses her, and I turn away because the last thing they need is an audience. The love they share for each other is what I like to think Ryley and I have. It's easy and unassuming.

"EJ is upstairs and ready for bed."

"Thanks Lois… for everything," I say, as I head upstairs. When I get to Grace's room, the kids are curled up together, sound asleep. I watch the rise and fall of EJ's chest. He's living in a peaceful world without any idea of what's going on around him. I have to protect him from what lies ahead and I'm confident that despite everything, Evan will do the same because the last thing he wants is to see his son hurt.

I hate to wake him, but I need to hold him tonight. He's my glue. His love repairs what ails me. I need him in my life and giving him up isn't an option. If Evan takes him away from me, I don't know what I'm going to do.

Scooping him up, I bring him into what's going to be my room for the foreseeable future. The sparsely decorated room already holds our bags, waiting to be unpacked. That will have to wait until tomorrow. Tonight, I'm going to lie in a bed that's not mine, holding my son and dreaming of how our lives were a month ago so that I can have a little semblance of what happy is again.

chapter 12
Evan

LAST NIGHT, WHEN RYLEY WAS standing next to me, I thought for sure we were over before we were given the chance to really start again. Still, her asking me to find a place to stay while she works out what she needs to do didn't hurt me as much as it shocked me. I didn't want to ask about Nate because it wouldn't matter how I phrased the question, it would have sounded childish and that's the last thing I want to be. But she knew it was on my mind and volunteered the information. Nate is going to go stay with Carter for a while and that made me as happy as I can be considering the situation.

As much as I don't want to give her the space she's asking for, I know I have to. I can't ask her to be something she's not ready to be, and if that means she needs time for her and EJ to figure out where they belong then so be it. She knows how I feel and I have no doubt she knows how Nate feels as well.

After I left Magoo's, I sucked it up and went back to

River's place. It was either that or the barracks and going back to base really doesn't appeal to me right now. River was waiting for me, which led me to believe that Ryley had called Frannie. Not only was I angry that she asked me not to come back to the house until everything could be sorted, but I became even more pissed that she shared this with my boss's wife. Honestly, it's something I should've expected. I just wasn't mentally prepared to hear the words come out of her mouth.

Sitting down in my favorite, yet most uncomfortable chair, Doc Howard sits opposite me while Ryley is to my left. Today is a therapy day and it couldn't have come at a better time. Last night I asked Ryley if she would come with me. I figured we could use today to discuss our newfound living situations and hopefully the good doc can provide some guidance. I thought Ryley would tell me she doesn't need help anymore, but she said she'd come for me. I really want her to be here for *us*, but we still have a lot to figure out.

"Good morning," Doc Howard says. Everything about her is like a bad routine – from the way she sits to the way she folds her hands. It's been about a week since I've seen her last, but expected with all the changes going on in my life she would change as well. As I sit here and look at her I realize I'm not being fair to her. I can't let my lack of sunny disposition affect my treatment.

She hasn't done me wrong yet.

"Morning, Doc," I say as I look at her then quickly to Ryley, who just smiles. I know Ryley doesn't like coming here, but it's a necessity. Not only do I need her here for emotional support, she fills in some of the holes. Lately, I've felt like it would have almost been better if I had lost my memory. I imagine thinking someone ruined my life on purpose is a far worse feeling than knowing I can't remember.

"Where do you want to start today, Evan?"

I take my eyes off Ryley and bring my focus in front of me. Inhaling deeply, I steel myself for the gasp I'm about to hear, but there's no use avoiding the thing that needs to be said. "Nate came home and Ryley kicked us both out."

The gasp is barely audible, but I hear it. Out of the corner of my eye I watch as Ryley clutches the armrest. She's angry and I get that. Could I have said it better? Probably, but I'm not going sugarcoat my feelings because she's sitting next to me. She should know that.

"Well that's definitely a change from last week. Let's talk about Nate first. Have you sat down and spoken with him, Evan?"

"No," I answer adamantly.

Doc Howard leans forward with her hands clasped in front of her. Her expression alone tells me that she doesn't approve.

Ryley clears her throat and sits a bit taller in the chair. "Nate only returned yesterday. In Evan's defense, they haven't had much of a chance to sit down."

"Don't need to."

"Evan," Ryley scolds.

"What? Unless he's going to tell me why he left me in the jungle so he could take over my life, we have nothing to discuss."

"You're being childish."

I want to throw my hands up in the air, kick my chair across the room and show Ryley just how childish I can be. Instead, I wrap my hands tightly around the armrests and squeeze them until the pressure builds and the pain starts to lessen.

"Ryley, why don't you tell me what happened yesterday?" Doc Howard asks in her calm, motherly voice.

She takes a deep breath and recounts our day at the beach. "Everything was perfect and that should've been my first clue that something was wrong. Evan was carrying EJ and I didn't even realize the door was already unlocked when I went to open it. The moment I saw Nate my heart sank and not because I didn't want Nate to be home, but because my time with Evan was going to change. For the past few weeks we've been together every day, as a family, and now that's going to be non-existent.

"The man I'm engaged to was sitting on the couch staring at us like we were aliens. EJ went straight to Nate as soon as he saw him. I know Evan felt broken when that happened because I felt that way for him," Ryley pauses and wipes at her cheek angrily. I didn't even know she was crying, her voice never gave any indication. Once again, I'm torn. Do I pull her into my lap and promise to take her pain away, or do I sit here and take it like a man? Why can't both be the answer?

"I asked Evan to leave last night so I could talk to Nate. I know Evan is never going to understand the relationship I have with his brother, but I owe it to both of them to be honest. Nate knows how I feel about Evan, he's always known. He accepts that I'll always love Evan. Even when we thought he had died, I never stopped loving him and the feeling only grew stronger the day he walked back into my life. I asked Nate and Evan to move out last night because I need space. I need time to myself to figure out what's right for me and EJ. I need to be able to think without either of them staring at me, asking me how I'm doing because the truth is, I don't even know right now.

"I wish there was a book full of answers or that Magic 8 Ball I had when I was kid actually worked, but neither are realistic. Everything is so screwed up and I hate that I'm hurting the two men that I love like this."

At hearing her words, I know what I have to do and I do it without hesitation. Ryley's in my arms before Doc Howard can even unclasp her hands to hand her a tissue. I nuzzle her neck, whispering that everything will be okay. The last thing I want in life is to hurt her and if me being here is causing her pain, I'll let her go, but not without a fight.

"Evan," Dr. Howard interrupts our moment. Ryley sits back in her chair, but I don't take my eyes off of her.

I clear my throat and prepare myself for whatever may come my way before speaking. "I spend a lot of time thinking. When Ryley and EJ are sleeping, I'm awake. I go over the orders we were given in my head. I think about letters that I received from her and had to burn; I have them memorized and go over them in my mind, looking for clues, even though I know she didn't write them. But I keep thinking maybe there was there something in there to alert me and I missed it.

"And then I start to wonder if our love wasn't strong enough for her to wait for me like Frannie did for River. I question everything and don't want to. All I can think is that I didn't love her hard enough, or long enough, for her to wait for me. Thing is, deep down I know that's not true.

"When Ryley was in college and I lived on base, the guys would go out and bring back a barrack bunny or two. They gave me such shit for being faithful and I'd tell them that when you're in love no one compares. I never questioned what I was feeling for Ryley. This woman completes me. She keeps me safe from myself.

"I want to believe that I'll prevail, but at what cost? The last thing I want to do is hurt Ryley or EJ. I wish there was a simple answer - a test you could give us to see who she's supposed to be with but I know that's not realistic so I keep trying to make sense of it in my head. Never in a million years did I think my competition would be my brother, but he is. And as much as it pains me to say this, if she doesn't choose me, and decides that Nate is the better choice, at least I know him. At least I can trust that he's not going to hurt her or my son."

"He loves me," Ryley says through tears.

I nod, knowing that's the truth. "Doesn't mean I have to accept it or honor it."

Doc Howard offers us a break and we both take it. I grab us some water, brushing my fingers along Ryley's hand as she takes the glass from me. Leaning in, I kiss her cheek. She pushes against me lightly and I use this to my advantage. Kissing her along her jaw, I whisper that I love her before I continue to pepper her skin with my lips. "So much," I tell her against the nape of her neck. I stop myself from asking her to never leave me. It's unfair and I know she won't be able to placate me.

Taking advantage of the room being empty except for us, I ask her, "When can I see you?"

"Tonight," she says as her green, teary eyes meet mine. "I'm not going to keep a schedule, Evan. There are no rules to all of this, but I *am* going to be fair."

"Are you going to sleep with him?" The words are out of my mouth before I can stop them, not that I would have. It's been on my mind and I have to know even if her answer tears my beating heart out of my chest.

Ryley shakes her head. "No, I'm not. And I'm not sleeping with you either."

That's what she thinks.

chapter 13
Nate

ONE NEVER SITS DOWN AND thinks about the "What If's" in life until it's too late to do anything about it. If I had, I likely wouldn't be sitting in a chair on my best friend's back porch contemplating them now.

What if I asked more questions about Evan's death?

What if I demanded more evidence that the burnt corpse with the missing limbs was my brother?

What if I didn't reenlist and Cara and I stayed together?

What if I never fell in love with Ryley?

What if this is all a set-up?

Then it begs the question, why? What did Evan and the other guys do to deserve this? The sliding glass door opens and Lois walks out with a tray of drinks. Always the consummate homemaker, she quit her job when Grace arrived so she could stay home with her. Grace and EJ will start school in the fall and Lois has mentioned going back to work part-time. She sets the tray down and hands me a tall, cool glass of lemonade.

Hope soars that it's spiked with something powerful, a numbing agent to quell my emotions, but as I take my first sip I realize it's just lemonade and only meant to quench my thirst on this hot summer day.

"You know I could give you a big ole song and dance on how everything is going to work out, but we both know it'll be a crock."

This is what I love about Lois, straight to the point and no hiding behind bullshit. She knows, just as I do, that this situation is beyond normal. People don't come back from the dead, and the people you trust to tell you the truth don't hide the fact that a member of your family is alive and well.

"She kicked me out." I hate the way the words sound as I say them. Ryley didn't kick me out, she asked me to leave. There's a difference, right?

That's what I'm telling myself.

Lois reaches for my hand and I let her hold it. "Ryley is going through a lot right now," she says, reconfirming everything I know. I can't begin to imagine the hell she went through when Evan showed up out of the blue.

"What am I going to do?"

Lois squeezes my hand before letting go. "If we had the answers, none of this would be happening. I know it's not easy for anyone, but you have to let her make the best decision for her and EJ without letting your own feelings get in the way."

I look at Lois questioningly. "You mean no guilt trips on how I was the one who was there for her and picked up the pieces?"

Lois chuckles and shakes her head. "You were going to be her brother-in-law. You should've been there to pick up the pieces regardless. But yes, no guilt trips. She has plenty of guilt for both you and Evan."

"I love her, Lois," I throw out there, even though she knows this.

"And she loves you, but she also loves Evan. When she finally opened herself up to you it was with the knowledge that Evan was never coming home. Same goes for you – you never would've pursued her if there was a chance that Evan was alive."

"Oh, I don't know about that," I say, chuckling lightly. In high school I wanted to pursue her, but shied away. Evan made it clear that Ryley was his. At first, I thought he'd use her and toss her away, but days turned into weeks, weeks into months and those months quickly turned into declarations of love, prom, and then basic training. The writing was on the wall, but I couldn't read it clearly.

In hindsight, I wish I had. I wouldn't be sitting here, staring off into the horizon, wondering what the hell has happened to my life.

"Did Evan know that you liked Ryley in high school?"

"He knew. It was instant, much like his attraction for her. He made it clear though, and I didn't fight him. Maybe I should've. I don't know." I shrug. "Thing is, I've never denied that they have a connection. She was the first girl that ever tamed him and she did it without trying. I remember a party we went to and for some reason Ryley couldn't go. As soon as we walked in girls were all over him and he ignored them, brushed them off, while I stood there, his twin, and they didn't even notice me. We look alike yet I couldn't get one girl to look in my direction."

Leaning forward, I let out a groan and scrub my hands over my face. "I don't mean to act like this. I just hate thinking about everything." I sit upright again, crossing my legs at my ankles. "This isn't a pity party. I'm happy that Evan's home, but I'm damn pissed about the whole situation. With our technology, how does this happen? We're trained to be the best, to get out of any situation possible and four guys who are presumed dead for six years just come waltzing back as if nothing's happened? How?"

Lois sets her hand on my forearm, a gentle reminder that she's here for me. "We've all been asking the same thing every day." She clears her throat. "I've called the news stations and the papers. Every time I think someone is interested in the story, they stop returning my emails and phone calls."

I turn sharply and face her. I can't get it out of my head that this is a cover up, but for what? My plan is to spend some time in the library and look at the old newspapers around the time that Evan left to see if anything looks suspicious. Thing is, I don't know what I'm looking for until Evan confides in me. Right now, the only thing I can get from him is anger, but his anger is misplaced.

"Was there a parade? Anything?"

Lois shakes her head slowly. "Nothing. There was one article by a no name journalist, but when I called the paper they told me that he's never worked there."

"Ryley said that Evan and the other guys received care packages?"

"Yeah, Evan had a picture of EJ from when he was a baby. He knew his name and everything. Evan knew things about them, everything except for where you were concerned."

Sighing deeply. "That must've gone over well."

"As well as getting your heart torn out of your chest would."

85

Which is exactly what's happening now.

It's been years since I've been in a library and if it weren't for the nice librarian I'd still be standing at the door scratching the back of my head. I'm grateful that she took pity on me and showed me what I needed. Sally, that's her name, set me up in the small, private room that holds the microfiche machine. After I left Lois sitting on the deck, I drove around until I found a library with this machine. I figured using the web would alert someone. If this was a set up, I don't want to leave a paper trail.

I start about six months before Evan left, going over every inch of the *Times*. I stay away from our local paper due to the fact they may not pick up on any international conflicts. I don't know what I'm looking for, but I'm looking. I'm just hoping that I'm not bypassing anything. The answers are out there, they just have to be found.

After a month of articles I realize that I'm not going to get anywhere unless I talk to Evan. He has answers whether he knows it or not, and the least he can do is give me something to go on. Everything Lois told me doesn't add up. My brother and his crew shouldn't be able to walk down the street without being mobbed by the media. Someone is keeping this quiet, but why? Where did they go? And what did they witness?

Article after article, note after note... everything I read and write down makes me think that I've lost my Goddamn mind. The sheer amount of possible situations could lead me anywhere and nowhere at the same time. I'm out of my league. I don't know what I'm doing.

Groaning in frustration, I flip forward to last month. The lone article that Lois told me about earlier is front and center. How I got so lucky and stopped the machine in this location,

I'll never know, but I'll take it.

No happy homecoming for SEALs declared dead by Navy
Art Liberty

SAN DIEGO – We have all seen and read about the happy homecomings of military members returning from deployment. Tearful but smiling family members embrace uniformed moms, dads, sons and daughters and welcome them back into their loving arms. High-ranking military and political officials give speeches lauding the bravery of the returning men and women. Sometimes there is even a band playing cheerful and patriotic music.

That is the joyful scene that we have become used to seeing on the Internet, television, social media, and newspapers. But that was not the welcome home reportedly experienced by four members of Navy SEAL Team Three, based in Coronado, CA.

They deplaned after a long flight from their theater of operations to be met by – no one. Instructed to take taxis from the airfield, the SEALs made their own way home to families that were anything but overjoyed to see them. The reason? All four were dead, according to the Navy. Funerals had been held with full military honors. "Taps" was played, a rifle salute was performed, and in a meaningful ritual peculiar to the Navy's elite warrior SEALs, fellow SEAL team members removed their Trident insignia and embedded it into the lid of the casket in a poignant and symbolic goodbye to a fallen brother-in-arms.

Sources close to the four men report that the SEALs, deployed for an unheard of six years, were regularly provided with "care packages" purportedly from their families at home, including items such as newsy letters and family photographs. The men are reportedly devastated by the thought that their loved ones believed them to be dead and buried for the past several years.

Lcdr. Becca Dawn, spokesperson for the Naval Special Warfare Command in Coronado, the command with authority over all Naval Special Warfare forces, said four days ago, "I am not aware of this issue or these men. I will have to get back to you." So far there has been no further comment and Lcdr. Dawn has not returned numerous messages. Several attempts were made to contact the Public Affairs Officer of Naval Special Warfare Group One, the parent command immediately over SEAL Team Three, have also not been returned. Former Navy Lt. Candy Brotz, past spokesperson for the command and now a reporter for *Military News* noted, "It is unheard of for SEALs to be deployed for that length of time. The circumstances are not only unusual, they are highly suspicious. The Navy doesn't just tell families that their sailor is dead without a lot of documentation and investigation."

Clearly this incident calls for answers from Navy authorities. Meanwhile, four traumatized families and four brave warriors try to rebuild shattered lives, if that is even possible.

Grabbing my pencil, I jot down Lcdr. Dawn and Lt. Brotz as people I need to contact. Brotz may know something and if she won't tell me, she might tell Carole. I read the article again, memorizing it word for word. How this article didn't prompt an investigation or media shit storm, I'll never know. Either way, I'm going to find these people, along with Art Liberty, and find out what the hell is going on.

chapter 14
Evan

IMAGINE MY SURPRISE WHEN I show up at Ryley's to spend a nice evening with her, only to find a note taped to the door directing me to Magoo's and reminding me that I need to get a cell phone. As much as I love the bar, it's not where I want to spend what little time I have with her. I was really hoping for a nice quiet dinner, maybe a romantic walk on the beach, followed by some serious adult time. But no, my girl wants to hang out at the bar of all places.

The thought crosses my mind that Ryley may be trying to re-create the life we had before some fucker decided to screw with us. We'd meet at Magoo's after work, hang out with friends and sometimes Cara and Nate would join us. Cara... the more I think about what's happened and my need to find the truth the more Cara enters into my thoughts. I could ask Ryley what happened between Cara and Nate, but I'm not sure my ego could take it if I found out she was the cause of them breaking up.

As soon as I walk in, I'm taken back to seven, eight years ago... to the last time I came home from deployment. That homecoming was a little happier, but this one could be just as nice. In the middle of the room, under a sign welcoming me home is the girl that I have loved for years. She stands there facing me, with a smile big enough to light up New York City. Some may think this is my moment to shine, but it's not, it's Ryley's. Welcome home parties aren't always for us, but for our families. It gives them a moment to finally breathe because they finally have us home. They finally get back to living life the way it's meant to be. Nothing is put on hold when we're home.

Surrounding Ryley are River and Frannie, my mom and Livvie, McCoy, Rask, Slick Rick, and Nate. If the sign didn't have my name on it, I'd wonder if this party was for him, too, since Carter, Lois and what looks like a few of his team are here. Ryley steps toward me and I look for any hesitation, the slightest inclination that she's only going to be friendly. She pauses before she reaches me, but I don't give her the opportunity to step back. I grab her, pulling her by her waist and pressing her flush against my body, kissing her deeply. A hush falls over the bar, not that I care. I know she's engaged to my brother unless she's called it off and this is really a party to celebrate that fact.

When she pulls away she bites her lower lip. I use this to my advantage and run my thumb over it pulling it free. "Welcome home, Archer," her words are barely audible and are only meant for me.

"As long as I'm with you, I'm home." Leaning down, I place a chaste kiss on her lips before looking over at my friends. "Where are your parents?"

"Someone had to watch EJ and they volunteered."

I appreciate it but wish they were here. They're the only ones who have treated me like a real person and not a ghost since I've been home. Our homecoming should've been different and I can only imagine that my team members are feeling a little bit somber. With Ryley's hand in mine I greet my friends and thank them for coming. When we get to my mother, I kiss her on the cheek.

"It's good to see you again, Mom."

"Yes well, Nate called and invited me." My eyes meet his over the top of my mother's head. His face is red, his jaw is clenched and the anger is rolling off him. Letting go of Ryley's hand, I place my arm around her shoulder and pull her into me. She stumbles a little, but regains her footing quickly. I know what I'm doing is probably wrong in a lot of people's eyes, but in mine, this woman belongs to me and I belong to her. I don't want to pretend when I'm with her.

"Mom, you remember Ryley, my fiancée and the mother of my son?"

My mother stiffens and Livvie steps away. The line is clearly divided where Livvie is concerned. I'm her favorite. I've known that for years, but she still looks up to Nate. While Nate and I aren't allowed to live with Ryley, Livvie is. It's my hope that my sister has come to her senses where Ryley is concerned. If not, I won't hesitate to pack up her shit and sending her back to my mother's.

"I believe she's engaged to Nate now. Am I right, Ryley?" She cocks an eyebrow at Ryley before looking down and away as if Ryley isn't worth the time it would take for her to respond. "And let's not forget about EJ," she says before turning her back on me.

"Huh, imagine that... my own mother wants to believe that my son belongs to you," I say to Nate before turning toward the bar. Ryley keeps stride with me until we reach the bar.

"So how does this work, Ry? Do I get one night and he gets the other? Or do we share nights, like tonight? Because if that's the case, you can pretty much guarantee that I won't be the third wheel on your dates."

Ryley rolls her eyes before squaring herself. "Do you love me?"

"You know I do," my reply is instant and factual, but gives me pause. Maybe I'm not saying it enough to her.

"Then shut up with your stupid comments. Your family and friends are here to celebrate your homecoming, which frankly should've happened weeks ago. I'm trying here and I need you to just accept what I'm offering until I can offer more."

Pulling her into my arms, I tell her that I'm sorry and that I do love her, more than anything in this world. I remind her that she's the reason I'm alive right now.

Rick hands us each a beer. As I bring mine to my lips, I watch her. She's uncomfortable with my question, but I'm not about to play nice. Nate shouldn't be at my party, not under the circumstances. The fact that he's here, knowing that I'll refuse to keep my hands off Ryley, is really pretty dumb on his part. He must love being tortured. Lord knows I wouldn't allow it.

"I'm going to go talk to Frannie," Ryley murmurs, letting her hand linger on my arm. I shake my head and watch her walk away. I don't know why she continues this charade of not knowing who she wants to be with. My brother is in the room and she doesn't hesitate to touch me. If I were Nate, I'd be livid. I wouldn't be standing there with our mother, whining to her as if she's going to do something about us not getting along.

Leaning back against the bar I survey the scene. Rask is in the corner flirting with a blonde while McCoy sits in the corner by himself. Empty beer mugs litter his table with a half empty one resting in his hand. My own problems have overshadowed his. In most cases, he's worse off. At least Ryley was in the same house when I came home. I need to be a better friend to him and help him find Penny and Claire.

River and Frannie are laughing at something Ryley is saying, which makes me smile. I don't even know what she's talking about, but a part of me feels as if I'm over there with them right now. A tap on my shoulder causes me to turn. Rick has placed a fresh beer down for me. I glance quickly at River to see if he's drinking. I'll need a ride home tonight because I don't plan on stopping as long as Nate is in the room.

Speaking of my brother, he and my mother, along with Carter and Lois grab a table to hold their "how-do-we-get-Evan-out-of-here-pow-wow". They're laughable, really, if they think I'm going to step aside and let Nate continue his takeover of my life.

Ryley walks by and I grab her by the waist, pulling her to me. I love it when her hair is down and I show her just how much by nuzzling her neck. God, she smells amazing. I've never been able to describe what she smells like, but her perfume drives me crazy and makes me want her even more. I nip at her ear, pulling her lobe in between my teeth. "I love you," I whisper as I brush the stubble on my face from her ear over her cheek. Capturing her lips, our tongues meet in a familiar dance, one that I've missed and so desperately need in order to live.

"What the fuck do you think you're doing?" Angry words are thrown at me as she's ripped from my arms. The last vision I have is of Ryley's face masked in fear. Her hands are covering her mouth, and I can't console her because my brother is standing in front of me.

"Do you have a problem, little brother?"

The bar falls silent as Nate's nostrils flare and his chest puffs out. I set my beer on the stool next to me so that I can keep my eyes on my enemy. I right myself, standing tall.

"You just don't get it do you?"

I'm sure I do, but I'm not willing to give him an inch. Picking up my beer, I take a nice long drink before setting it down again. Smacking my lips together, I smirk. "Why don't you fill me in?"

Nate takes a step closer and points his finger at me. My eyes never leave his. "You need to respect the ring on her finger."

I chuckle and shake my head. "Just like you respected the one I left there?" I cock my eyebrow at him, watching as his face turns redder.

"You left her." His words rip through me. His lies tear at my heart.

"The fuck I did," I roar as my fist flies, connecting with his jaw. The satisfying sound of a crack has me rearing back for another punch. Nate stumbles, but doesn't touch the side of his face. He's a warrior after all. Ignoring the screaming, I charge forward, only to be knocked back when his fist connects with my nose. My eyes water, but that doesn't stop me from pursuing my enemy, from annihilating my competition.

Strong arms circle round me like a vice grip, holding me

back. Nate steps closer, his lip bleeding as a result of my hit. "Come at me, fucker," I say as I spit in his direction.

Carter steps up to Nate, his hand on his chest. "Be the bigger man. Don't stoop to his level."

"That's right, Nate, don't covet what isn't yours," I say only I'm looking at Carter. He returns my glare and shakes his head. I don't care for nor do I need his approval.

"Come on man, let's take a walk." It's McCoy who's holding me back. He shoves me toward the door, but not before I make eye contact with my family. My mother is showing her disapproval by glaring at me. Livvie's eyes are going from me to Nate, and Ryley is crying. I made her cry again. Maybe that should be my sign, my clue that she's better off with Nate and not me.

We fought when we were younger, but never like this and never over a girl. Hell, I've never fought for a girl. Never had to. But for Ryley, I'd fight to the death. I'm not sure she understands that about me.

For her, I'd lay down my life.

McCoy hangs on to me until we're around the side of the bar. The sea air is somewhat refreshing over the smell of stale beer and embedded cigarette smoke from when people could smoke in bars.

I slam my fist against the concrete wall a few times before McCoy pushes me away. "Take a walk," he tells me. His voice is gruff, demanding. He knows me. He knows what I'm capable of. I walk away with my hands linked behind my head. McCoy lingers near me and for what? Maybe save me from myself? Or save me from Nate? It doesn't matter which scenario it is because right now, I'm a ticking time bomb.

"Can you believe him?" I ask, throwing my hands up in

the air.

McCoy shakes his head slowly. "Nope, but I can't believe you either."

"What are talking about?"

He pushes his hands into his pockets and looks at me. "I get that you're angry and pissed off. Hell, I'm in the same sinking boat you are. We got fucked and there ain't a single person willing to help us out. But Ryley moved on and you have to respect that shit. Would you be this pissed if it was some other guy?"

His question stings, but he's right. If Ryley had moved on with someone else I would have to suck it up and just deal with it, but she didn't. She moved on with my brother and that's something you just don't do.

"I'd have my son, McCoy. I'd have the part of her that we created together. But right now, my boy thinks another man is his father and I don't see that man telling my son otherwise."

"So tell him yourself; you're entitled."

"Please don't." We turn at the sound of Nate's voice not far behind us. Our training should've alerted us to the fact that he was there, but I'm too angry to even notice my surroundings. And hearing Nate ask me not to tell my son that I'm his father when I'm already this pissed off does not bode well for him at all.

chapter 15
Nate

"Please don't." The words are out of my mouth before I can stop them. It's not how I meant to start the conversation, but after hearing McCoy suggest that Evan tell EJ the truth, it's the only thing I could say. It's not that I don't want EJ to know. I actually think he *should* know. I just can't figure out how to go about telling him.

I look down at the bag of ice in my hand, my peace offering. It's not much, but what just happened in there, in front of our friends and family, can't happen again. We aren't Neanderthals. We're family and you don't treat family this way.

Evan is going to say the same thing to me and he's right. The way I behaved after he died... I should've known better. I let my heart get in the way of what's right and wrong and now a five-year-old boy is going to pay the price because the adults in his life can't make the proper decisions.

"McCoy, do you think I could speak with Evan?" Kill 'em with kindness. That's what my father used to say. But he'd also remind us to never show our opponent any weakness. Ryley and EJ are the Archers' weakness.

Evan stands facing McCoy and with his back to me, only the floodlights of the bar illuminating the area. They have a silent exchange. Something only brothers you have been to battle with would be privy to. It's my hope that Evan will open up to me about his time away. That he'll let me help him.

As soon as McCoy walks away, Evan turns. I toss the bag of ice at him. "It's a peace offering," I say in hopes to break the proverbial ice. "Look, what happened in there… we need to come to an understanding."

"No, what we need to do is decide when EJ finds out I'm his father."

"I'm not out here to fight with you."

"Afraid you'll lose?" he asks, his tone mocking.

"No, it's not that," I answer with a shake of my head. "I'm concerned about where you've been and I think you need to hear me out about what life has been like the past six years."

I walk over to the picnic bench and sit down. I remember when Rick put this out here, thinking that we'd want to sit and relax. A few did, but being inside is where the ambience is. Inside is where we feel like we can relax and let our guard down just a little bit.

"What you were doing in there was low. You know she's my fiancée, and yet you had no qualms about kissing her."

Evan shrugs. "You had no qualms taking over my life, so I guess we're even."

I should've known that talking to him at all wouldn't be easy but talking about Ryley and EJ is probably going to be an extremely tumultuous conversation. Maybe she should be here to referee, but putting her in the middle of any more disagreements between us is the last thing I want to do. She loves us both and I wish none of us were going through this.

"I'm not going to sugar coat anything. The other day when you walked in, I thought I was looking at a ghost and part of me is still waiting for you to disappear. And if I'm being honest, I'm not sure you're even you. I mean you look like you and Ryley says it's you, but I can't wrap my head around a crew of Navy SEALs being gone for six years without being prisoners of war, or missing in action. None of this shit makes sense, Ev, and I'm trying to get a clear picture.

"I know coming home was a shock, but you have to understand when I tell you that Ryley and me ending up together wasn't planned. I didn't set out to be with her. Things just happened. Our feelings developed over the years and we acted on them. We shared a bond. One of the things you said the other day really made me think a lot: How does it feel to be you? And the answer is, I never set out to take over your life. I was happy with Cara and I was happy being an uncle to EJ.

"But when shit went south between Cara and me, I started spending more and more time over at Ryley's because she was my connection to you. Being at the cemetery where you're buried wasn't cutting it. I needed a connection and she and EJ were it. It was years, Evan, before she and I even discussed what we were feeling, because we were both afraid of tarnishing your memory."

Evan finally raises the bag of ice to his nose. He winces from the cold sensation and pressure being applied to his face.

"I hate you."

"I know," I say, sighing heavily. "If I knew you were alive, I swear to God I would've been looking for you."

Evan sits down and, to me, this means progress. "That's

just it," he says as he leans forward, resting one of his elbows on his knee. His other hand is still holding the ice pack. "About three months in I asked O'Keefe to get a message to you. I wanted you to know that everything was good, but that I needed you to check on Ry because she was pregnant. He told me that he gave you the message. I left it at that because a few days later a box came from Ryley with pictures of her belly getting bigger and a letter."

"Was it her handwriting?" I ask the moment he pauses.

Evan shakes his head. "I never thought about it until now, but all her letters were typed and I think I figured at the time that she was tired and didn't want to handwrite everything."

"You were about fifty days out when they came knocking on the door. They told Ryley first before they told Mom or me. Ryley called me and I could hear it in her voice when she said your name. By the time I got to your house, Carole and Jensen were there and Carole was on the phone yelling at someone. I had never seen her scream before that day. That was also the day Ryley told me she was pregnant. I didn't know what to think until Mom came storming in, demanding that Ry move out."

Evan groans, and I know why: Our mother. When our father died, she changed. She became cold and shut off. It's not that I blame her, but she still had three children that needed her. When Evan died, she became mechanical and shut off. EJ has brought her back a little, but not much. To him, she's an amazing grandmother. To the rest of us, she's cold hearted.

"Mom begged Carole to investigate and she did. I know she spent hours scouring through documents looking for something that would tell us otherwise, but every 'T' was crossed and all the 'I's' were dotted. Whoever wanted you guys to disappear did a damn fine job of covering the trail."

Taking a deep breath, I try to relax against the wooden table, but it's old and splintered, the fragmented wood poking me in the back as I look out over the parking lot and the beach volleyball court.

"What were you doing? Where'd you go?"

The moment I ask the question, the door to Magoo's opens. I catch a glimpse of someone stepping out, but that's it. They're staying close to the wall because if they step out from under the awning, the floodlights will come on. "Stop talking," he mumbles.

"Why?" We need to hash this shit out and now is the best time. We could've killed each other in the bar. I'm not walking away from this now.

"It's Frannie," he whispers.

Glancing back toward the door, I'm still waiting for whoever came out to come into view. "How do you know?"

Evan leans back, resting his arms on the top of the table, letting his bag of ice dangle from his hand. "It's her perfume. After being at River's for a day, I'd recognize it anywhere."

His statement gives me pause. He's on high alert, something I'm not. I'm not sure I'd be able to pick out Lois's perfume if she walked out of the bar under the cover of darkness, but Evan knew right away. And something about Frannie being outside by herself has him on edge.

"We still need to talk," I say, keeping my voice low. Evan sighs heavily and groans.

"Listen," he says, back to resting his elbows on his knees. "Right now the only thing I want is my son. He needs to know I'm his dad. I don't care what telling him does to the relationship you and Ryley have with him. I don't care what the reasoning is behind the decision to never tell him about me, and thinking that my face tacked to his walls was the answer. That shit is creepy and cool at the same time, but he needs to know and I'm not waiting." Evan stands and starts to pace, kicking pebbles as he does. I know he's right, and it's not that I don't want to do what he's asking, I just don't know how. It's also a decision I can't make without Ryley.

It doesn't escape my notice that he says he only wants EJ. I know he wants Ryley, and it makes me think that maybe she's told him no. If she has, she hasn't said anything to me about it. She's asked for space and I'm giving it to her.

"I want to help," I say, without going into detail. His head turns toward the building where I'm assuming Frannie is lurking. Evan tosses the bag of ice on the table and groans.

"Help what? Help tell EJ that I'm his father? Help by leaving Ryley so she and I can be together? Help figure out what the fuck happened to us?" The last question he says a little more loudly, making me wonder if he thinks Frannie is involved.

"Evan?"

He puts his hand up. "Not here, not now." He walks away before I can respond. If not now, when? We can't put this off, lives and feelings are going to get in the way of any resolve that we can muster if we do.

"Hey Frannie, are you getting some fresh air?"

"Oh, hey Evan, didn't know you were out here."

My blood turns cold at their conversation. Evan was right, not that I doubted him, but her response doesn't make sense. Everyone in that bar saw what happened. She had to know that the both of us were out here.

My head pounds as the sunlight filters through the blinds. After my talk with Evan last night, Carter and I decided that the best medicine for a busted lip and slightly bruised ego was to get shitty drunk. I'm paying for it today though. Glancing quickly at my phone, it's just after noon. It's been years since I've slept the day away and damn it if I don't feel like I haven't even slept yet.

Sitting on the edge of the bed, my hands hold my head to keep the room from spinning. Today is going to suck and as much as I want to blame Evan and his wandering lips, he's not the reason I started drinking. Life is. Not long after Evan went back into the bar, he left by himself. Ryley chased after him but came back alone. I tried not to let her eagerness to be with him affect me, but I lost that battle. She should've been by my side and not his. I guess when you ask for space, you're allowed to do whatever you want.

The house is quiet when I walk down the stairs in desperate need of some aspirin and water. I'm never drinking again and that will last until the next time I'm feeling sorry for myself. As soon as I step into the living room the sight of the beautiful redhead who agreed to marry me a year ago catches my eye. Ryley sets her magazine down and smiles. Her sun-kissed shoulders are on full display with the tank top style, royal blue dress she's wearing.

"Good afternoon."

Running my hand over my recently shaved head, I groan

loudly and go to her. I curl up, resting my head on her leg, and moan. "I feel like shit." She laughs as her fingers move over my stubble.

"I know things aren't easy, Nate, but that's no reason to get wasted."

"Is that what Lois told Carter?"

This time she laughs loudly. "Lois made Carter get up and mow the lawn. Now he has both kids with him at the grocery store. She also told Grace that she could wake him up and she did it with music and high-pitched singing from what Lois said."

"That's pure torture."

"In the best form," she says as she leans forward, kissing me on the cheek. I turn before she can move and press my lips to hers. I hate sharing her, but I refuse to give up on the love we have. I deepen the kiss, pushing my fingers into her hair. Our kiss is slow and sweet. She makes me feel like I can accomplish anything when she's with me.

She rests her forehead against mine before sitting upright. I'm not stupid to think that everything is back to normal and that she's here to tell me that she's ready for me to come home. That would mean the nightmares I've been having are just that. That would also mean my brother isn't home, and I'd rather have the nightmares than have him gone again.

"We need to talk about EJ."

"I know," I say, as I sit up. I want to pick her up and take her upstairs. I want to crawl back under the covers and have us close our eyes and never have this conversation.

"It's not going to be easy."

My eyes water from the images in my mind of me telling EJ that I'm not his dad. If I had known Evan was still alive

I would've stopped EJ from calling me "Dad" all those years ago, but I didn't and my selfishness is coming back to bite me in the ass.

"None of this is easy, Ry. Our lives are so fucked up right now. We've made so many mistakes. The lies have been built and now we have to dig ourselves out of the hole without a shovel."

Ryley leans into me, clasping her hand with mine. "I don't have the answers, but I think we need to do it all together. We owe it to Evan to give him this. Regardless of you and me, or Evan and me, EJ's his son and they both need each other."

I nod, due to a lack of words. I know she wants to do this today, whereas I want to pretend it's never going to happen.

"I'll go shower," I kiss her on the forehead, letting my lips linger there. "When Carter's back, we'll call Evan and go meet him. We'll do this as a family and at someplace EJ loves so he can feel comfortable."

With that I leave her on the couch so I can get ready for the day. She'll never understand how much her words have hurt me and I'll never tell her. She's a woman being torn in half by two men, both of whom she loves for different reasons, both of whom want her for themselves.

chapter 16
Evan

It feels like I'm watching one of Ryley's romance movies play out in live action. Ryley's pushing EJ in the swing and I can hear him yelling, "Higher, higher!" Nate stands in front of the swing, but just enough out of the way so that he doesn't get kicked. When EJ descends, Nate is there to push him back toward Ryley. It's me who should be doing that with Ryley, but instead I'm sitting in my car watching like a stalker. I'm that guy you read about in the paper, hear about in the news, the man who lurks around public parks looking to snatch a wife and her kid so I can take them home to play house.

No... I hunt bastards like that.

I'm actually supposed to be here. Today's *the day* and I'm nervous as hell. I've faced death many times, but facing a five-year old and telling him that I'm his father and Nate isn't scares the ever-loving shit out of me. What if he rejects me? What if I'm not the father that Nate is, or I can't handle it? He's been able to learn as he goes, but a five-year old has expectations that I may not be able to meet.

A police officer stops next to my car and motions for me to roll down my window. I try not to roll my eyes, but I get it. Once my window is down, he leans over his console. The look on his face is telling me that he's not impressed that I'm sitting here staring at the people in the park.

"Wanna move along?"

Yes, as a matter of fact, I do because facing a five-year-old is scarier than facing a terrorist. "Just about to get out, sir."

He moves back and forth, trying to peer into my car. My guess is that he's checking for my family or my kid. Too bad he's looking in the wrong direction. He obviously doesn't perceive me as too much of a threat since he's still in his car.

"This is a family park," he says as his radio squawks. He answers in code before turning back to me. "Where's your family?"

Without taking my eyes off of him, I point to the swing set where Ryley and EJ are. Realization hits him like a ton of bricks and regardless of whether our return has been front and center in the paper or on the news, people know... he knows.

"You're the one who came home?"

"One of the four, yes sir." I'm not the only one who returned and each of us has to deal with our own fall outs in life, except for River. He just has to figure out why his wife had his beer stocked in his refrigerator. And not just stocked, but fresh, recently purchased and ready for his return. Who does that?

He nods and starts to say something but closes his mouth. Keeping my focus on him, I wonder if he's met the struggles that I have. Not likely, but as a police officer, each time he walks out of his house he expects to return when his shift is over. He doesn't know if there's a crazed lunatic waiting to wreak havoc on his day. His job is really no different from mine. He battles the locals while I - or *we* - take on the rest. To me, he's my partner.

"The community stands behind you, son," he says before he rights himself behind his steering wheel. As he drives away I keep my eyes on him, wishing he'd stay just a bit longer. Sometimes it's just nice to talk to someone who may or may not experience what you're going through. I can't talk to the guys because each of us is experiencing our return differently. Talking to Ryley produces heartache and shattered dreams. And my fear with Nate is that he'll use any information I might give him against me.

Taking a deep breath, I ready myself for what's about to happen. As it is, I'm already late, which is undoubtedly a strike against me. They'll never understand what this is like for me. Even though I've met my son, he thinks of me as a friend and I'm not foolish enough to think that today will be any different, but it'd be nice.

Walking across the park with my hands pushed deep into my pockets, I think about turning back. Since Ryley asked me to leave the house I've wondered if I'm in a parallel universe. My homecoming was supposed to be filled with family, love and acceptance, but it's been anything but. It took a therapist to convince her that I needed to be a part of EJ's life. She threw me a party, but not until after Nate came home. She tells me that she's not going to marry him, yet she still wears his ring and he seems to think that they're still together.

Stopping halfway, Nate pulls Ryley into a hug. He picks her up and twirls her around, something I've done many times, but not lately. EJ is loud when he tells Nate to do it again, adding "Daddy" to the end of his sentence. EJ loves them, as his parents, his family and I'm not sure I belong. To EJ I could be viewed as an intruder, someone he's not willing to accept as a parent. I guess I need to ask myself if I'm okay with that, or if I'm going to push him.

I have to avert my gaze. I can't look at them, happy and in love. The trees, the birds and even the other families that are in the park seem to be a better option for me right now. Turning around, my car sits on the side of the street ready to take me away. Maybe that's what I need, a destination far from here where I can start over and pretend that my life is everything that it isn't right now.

The laughter coming from the others is enough to tell me that I shouldn't be here. Right now, I have nothing to offer EJ and Nate does. He's offered him stability, a home and father, while I've been nothing more than pictures on his wall. He's better off with Nate, and at this point so is Ryley.

My steps are solid even though the ground has a bit of give to it. My legs feel heavy and slow moving, and short of running, I'm never going to get back to my car without them seeing me.

"Hey, Eban?"

My name and the excitement in his voice is enough stop me in my tracks. I turn to find the mini version of me staring back. He's wearing his own NWU pants with a matching hat.

"Hey, EJ." I don't know what else to say. I'm an adult and this little boy brings me to my knees.

"Are you my dad?"

My eyes widen at his question and I seek out Ryley and Nate who are sitting at a table not far from the swing sets. I sit down on the ground and EJ mimic's my position. How do you answer a question you're not prepared for? I thought I was until I got here, but now that he's in front of me I just want to tell him no because he'd be so much better without the drama that my life is right now.

"Um…" I hesitate but realize that he needs an answer. "Who told you that?" I ask as if I'm back in high school trying to figure out who started a rumor about me.

"My mom and dad," he says as he turns and looks over his shoulder, making sure they're still there.

"Right." They told him without me, but why? Was it to make things easier on me? Did they know I was going to have second thoughts about doing this? Or did they do it just to get it over with?

"Are you?" he asks again, growing impatient.

"I am, but do you know what that means?"

"Yes," he says, picking at the grass. "It means that you're the dad that helped make me, but my dad is the one who is helping me be a man. You know I'm going to be in the Navy, too."

I laugh even though I find nothing funny about this situation. It's not the Navy part that bothers me, but that he says Nate is the one who's helping him become the man he should be.

I want to be that person.

"I don't know how to talk to a five-year old," I tell him, thinking he probably doesn't understand me. "Listen EJ, I'm new at this and I'm going to make a lot of mistakes, but I love you and have loved you since you were just this little bean in your mommy's tummy. I was so excited when we found out you were coming, but I had to go to work. My job took a very long time to finish, but I'm here now and I want to be your dad. Does this make sense to you?"

"I dunno. Mom says that I can call you 'Dad' if I want."

My heart soars with anticipation until he speaks again and says, "But I like calling you Eban because it's the same name as me."

Swallowing hard, I try to ward off the emotions threatening to take over. I bring my knees to my chest, resting my arms over them and grabbing my wrist with my hand.

"Are you crying, Eban?"

"No," I shake my head. "My eyes are just sweating."

He laughs and I smile, but it's forced. Clearing my throat, I say, "Do you think that maybe you'll want to call me 'Dad' someday?"

He shrugs and places his picked grass onto his leg. "Do you think my dad will be mad?"

I want to be a damn child and yell at him, telling him that Nate is *not* his dad, but I'll save that for Ryley and Nate later.

Instead, I shake my head knowing I've not earned the right to say what I want where EJ's concerned, but realizing he doesn't know that. He doesn't know me. "I think he'll understand."

EJ briefly looks over his shoulder again. His little hand grabs a fist full of grass, pulling hard until he brings up clumps of dirt.

"Why do you look like my dad?"

"Why do you think you look like me?" I counter.

He shrugs. "I dunno."

I stop talking for fear that I'll say something stupid. I should've stayed at River's today. I should've never agreed to come to the park when Ryley called and invited me. I let River and Frannie encourage me and now here I am, confused and hurt. I feel empty and half of who I am on the inside. The love of my life is in love with a man I share DNA with and they're raising my son together whether I like it or not.

EJ stands and brushes off his legs. "See ya later, Eban." And before I can ask him to stay he's gone. He runs back to Ryley and Nate as if his ass were on fire. I'm watching him the whole way, fighting every urge to scream, kick, fight, run after him, cry and beg for him to just accept me as his dad.

As soon as I see Ryley heading in my direction, I stand and walk away. I don't want to talk to her, not today and probably not tomorrow. I may be a meathead, but I'm not stupid and I refuse to be treated as such. The writing is on the wall. She and Nate are going to stay together, my feelings be damned.

"Evan, wait."

"Can't, gotta go," I tell her, without stopping. Her hand pulls on my arm until she's standing in front of me.

"Where are you going?"

"Home. I mean River's. Away. What does it matter?"

She blanches at my answers and her eyes widen. They're the same beautiful green eyes that stared at me when she was lying on the ground after I hit her with the football. "What's going on?"

I shake from the anger coursing through my body right now. Her dumb act isn't lost on me. Pulling at the ends of my hair in frustration, I let out a loud groan.

"You told him without me being there! So, you and Nate decided that Nate will still be his dad and I'm what? That I'm some guy that comes by every now and again?" My voice is louder than I want, but I can't control it.

"No," she answers weakly, pissing me off even more.

113

"Then, what? I get it, Ry. I'm not stupid. You want to be with Nate, fine, be with him. But that little boy is my son and I'm going to be in his life. I know when to step aside and *this*... well, this is me walking away."

For the first time in my life I'm willingly walking away from the one girl I've loved my whole life. The one girl I never thought I'd be away from. The one girl who I thought would love me no matter what life threw at us.

chapter 17
Nate

"DO YOU HAVE EVERYTHING?"

Mom fusses, folding another t-shirt and placing it in the pile.

"Yes Mom, I do," Evan assures her. He's leaving before me by one week. We thought we'd be in basic together, but he enlisted after me and he told them that he plans to be a SEAL. The Navy plans to kick his ass.

"You can change your mind, you know." Mom has been telling him this every day since he signed his name on the dotted line. She didn't say it to me - maybe because this is something I've wanted for the last year. That's what I'm telling myself, at least.

Shaking those thoughts out of my head, I know I have to save Evan. I set my hand on her shoulder, butting in on his behalf. "Mom, he'll be fine. Just think, next week you can worry about me." I all but push her out of Evan's room and shut the door.

"I should kick your ass for leaving a week early," I tell him, sitting down in the chair at his desk. I pick up a picture of him and Ryley and smile. He loves her. If you had asked me nine months ago, I would've said it's not possible for Evan Archer to love anyone but himself.

"She's going to miss you," I say, setting the photo back down on his desk.

"She'll miss you, too."

"I'm talking about Ryley."

Evan sighs. I expected them to break up, but I've been proven wrong. This is a new side of my brother. He's heading to basic training with a girlfriend. It's either a crazy notion and they won't last, or he's going to be the biggest pussy-whipped sailor in the Navy.

"I need you to promise me something."

"Anything," I tell him without hesitation.

He walks over to me and pulls out his desk drawer. He picks up a white envelope and my heart drops. "If anything happens to me, ever, give this to Ryley."

"Evan?"

"No, just listen. I know you like her, Nate, but I love her. I'm going to marry her, but if at any time I don't make it back, you give her this letter and make sure nothing ever happens to her. Make sure she knows that I love her with everything that I am. I need you to promise me that you'll take care of her."

"I promise," I say, taking the letter from his outstretched hand.

I flip the yellowed worn paper between my fingers. It's fragile from years of being folded. I came over to Ryley's to give her a letter that I should've given her years ago, but sometimes it takes a word to bring back a memory from a time in your life when everything was perfect.

Evan said something the other night that reminded me of this letter. He gave it to me a few days before he left for basic training. He wrote it the night Ryley tried to break-up with him. He wouldn't let her. I don't blame him.

"What's going on?"

I follow her voice to find her standing in the doorway with

a laundry basket on her hip. She smiles, reminding me why I love her, but I can't help thinking that maybe we don't belong together. My brother loves her and part of me thinks I should step aside, but I know she loves me too.

"Come here," I say to her. She sets the basket down and walks over to me, holding her hand out for me when she gets close.

Curling up with her on the couch is my favorite thing to do. The quiet, the calm, especially after a crazy day at work, is all that I need. She and EJ give me solid footing and I know what to expect when I get home: Smiles, hugs and lots of laughs. But lately we haven't been laughing at all.

"What's that?" she asks, pointing to the envelope resting on my leg. My lips go into a thin line thinking that what I'm about to tell her could be the catalyst for our demise. Sighing, I put my arm around her and kiss her forehead.

"Evan gave this to me a long time ago. I forgot about it until the other day. I was supposed to give this to you if something happened to him. He wrote it the night you tried to break-up with him. He asked me before he left for basic to hold onto it and give it to you in the event something happened to him. I promised I would and I broke that promise... I'm not trying to make up for it now, but think you should probably read it."

Giving her the letter, I close my hand around hers. I have a sinking feeling that whatever he wrote on that piece of paper when he was eighteen is going to be enough to end us. It's my fault if that's the case. I should've given it to her years ago.

"I'm meeting your mom for lunch," I say, standing. Ryley and I have so much to discuss, but I don't want to be here when she reads what Evan has written. It's better for me that way. Decisions need to be made that are going to hurt.

Not her...

Not Evan...

They'll hurt me.

Yesterday at the park, Ryley and I made a mistake when we told EJ that Evan was his dad. We should've waited for him to be there with us, but there's no handbook on how to break the news about something like this. In that moment, we thought we were doing the right thing. In the end, we only hurt Evan and he's been hurt enough.

I don't know if I'm man enough to walk away from Ryley. I'm not sure I'm man enough to even try.

"Thanks for meeting me." Carole stands and offers her cheek, which I kiss lightly. She's dressed in black slacks and a white button down blouse, civilian clothing. It's different seeing her during the workday like this. Usually when I visit her at lunchtime she's in her Navy uniform, sitting behind her desk in the JAG office. Before I can sit down the waitress is at our table handing us menus and taking my drink order. Carole is already nursing a glass of Chardonnay and as much as I'd love a beer, I order water. I have a lot to talk about and need to keep my wits about me.

"I can understand why you didn't want to meet on base," Carole says, bringing her glass to her lips. "I'm not sure public is safe either, though."

"I know but home may not be the best option. Besides,

I'm staying with Carter and Lois, I don't want to impose."

"Are you afraid the house is bugged?" she asks, leaning forward to keep her voice down. My soon to be mother-in-law, unless Ryley decides to call off our engagement, is a conspiracy theorist. She's always looking for the underlying message in a story. Many times I've joked with her that if someone is going to uncover the truth, it's going to be her. I'm not joking anymore, though. The truth needs to come out. The only problem with getting Carole involved is that I'm afraid she'll lose her job... *or worse.*

"I'm not sure. I get the feeling that Evan thinks so, but we're not exactly on speaking terms right now. I need to find out what happened to him and why this is happening to us. Lois told me there has been only one article since they came home. One! And I don't think for a second that it's a coincidence that all of this happened days after we were sent out on a training exercise."

Pulling out a folded piece of paper, I slide it across the table toward Carole and start talking. "The guy who wrote this, Art Liberty, I can't find him. He doesn't work for the paper, or he did and isn't anymore. No phone, no email. It's like he doesn't exist. Lois told me that she called the news stations and the papers to get some coverage for Evan and no one would call her back. Four guys return from the dead and they get no air play, that right there tells me something is up."

"I read this article, but there was never any follow-up. I thought for sure this reporter would come around, but he never did - at least Ryley never said anything," Carole tells me.

Looking around, I bring my chair closer and lean in. "Do you know where Lcdr. Dawn is?"

"What do you mean?"

"I mean, I asked for her before calling you. She's not stationed in Coronado, or she's been transferred. I don't know, but no one has heard of her."

"I have," Carole states, relieving some of the anxiety that's building. "But I haven't seen her in a few weeks now that I think about it."

When the waitress is within eyesight I lean back in my chair, opening the menu to find something to eat. Carole orders first and I ask for a burger and fries. I'm not that hungry, but want people to think we're just having lunch. It's not odd for us to be out together, it's just never happened until now.

"I called the *Military News* to talk to Candy. She says she doesn't remember talking to this Liberty reporter."

"Do you think Liberty is a pseudonym for someone in the Navy?"

Shrugging and now wishing we were someplace more private, I lean in. "I don't know what to think except my brother is a walking, talking zombie. Someone knows something and they're not talking and the two people that did some talking are conveniently missing. Our lives are being turned inside out. Evan hates me, Ryley is confused and EJ is trying to grasp the fact that Evan is his dad. I want to know why this happened to my family."

"Do you think Evan witnessed something?"

"I don't know, Nate. I've been asking the same thing ever since Ryley called and told us he was home. I wouldn't have believed her had I not seen him for myself."

Carole and I separate when our food arrives. We both pick at our food, keeping our conversation limited to things like Ryley, EJ and family picnics. Every time the door chimes, I'm watching the people entering. Each one, to me, is a suspect in this bullshit mess. I just need to figure out where to start. Calling around and looking for people who may or may not exist isn't cutting it.

As soon as we're finished, I pay the tab and suggest that Carole and I take a walk. She happily agrees and takes my arm, earning some very dubious looks from the other patrons. Trying not to laugh at their expressions, I wink and receive the same scrutiny… If they only knew how much I admire the woman on my arm for everything that she's achieved in her career, not to mention that she's been like a second mom to me.

Carole keeps my arm until we're a block away from the café. The sun is out, warming the afternoon. I should be on base working, but finding out what's happened in the past six years is far more important. Tomorrow, I'm going to ask for personal leave. My request is likely going to be denied since my Team is being deployed, but there's no way I can leave right now. Whether Evan wants my help or not, I'm going to find out who did this.

As soon as we step into the park, Carole slips off her shoes. "My heels will get stuck in the grass," she explains.

"I wasn't judging," I respond, trying not to laugh.

"Let's find a bench. I want to talk freely." It takes us a few minutes until Carole is happy with one of the benches. She chooses one out in the open when I would've chosen one by the trees.

"Why here?" I ask, sitting down next to her.

"You can see everything and no one is able to lurk behind trees to listen to us speak."

Looking around I see that she's right.

"When the guys landed, they did so at an abandoned airfield and taxis were waiting for them. That's all public knowledge. What's not public is that their CO hasn't been seen or heard from since that day. He never returned to base. His phone is off and his credit cards haven't been used. A body was found four days ago, the same day you came home. The body is badly decomposed and was sent to the county morgue for identification. I have a friend in NCIS who did some digging. The body is now missing. I don't know if there's a connection, but it seems that everything can be connected to a timeline.

"Senator Lawson has been on base asking questions. He's from Florida and has been rumored to be putting his name in the mix for Presidency. He seems very interested in Team 3, but is very hush-hush when I'm around. I don't like it and I don't like him. He has no business here, especially in California politics. You and Evan are right to think that there's something not right about this, but I don't know what it is. And I want to talk to you about Rask.. He's on base, lingering. I know his family has written him off and he needs someone to talk to."

"He was at Evan's party the other night and seemed fine," I offer, but I honestly don't know him that well. He was new to Evan's team right before they left.

"Jensen isn't going to be happy with me, but I'm going to do what I can to help you and Evan. My daughter and grandson are the most important people in my life and I hate seeing them hurt so if I can find out what happened, I'm going to."

Shaking my head, I tell her, "It's not safe."

Carole turns and stares into my eyes pointedly. "None of us are safe, Nate." She looks over my shoulder before standing and walking away. Spinning in my seat I look around for who she saw, but don't recognize anyone. I search for Carole, but she's already out of sight, leaving me questioning everything she just told me.

chapter 18
Evan

My muscles burn, but it's a welcome pain. Each time I push the weighted bar, I'm rewarded with agony and I welcome it. I crave it. It's been years since I've been able to work out and I hadn't realized how much I've missed it until now.

My spotter, a trainer who works here, helps me finish my last rep before he walks away to tend to his next client. My chest heaves from exhaustion. I'm out of shape, my core is weak and being weak has no place in my life.

The punching bag is calling my name, begging me to take my aggression out on it. When Nate and I were younger, we'd spar. We'd get in the ring and work each other out. It was for exercise, not pain. I never wanted to hurt him until now. I used to have my own set of boxing gloves, but I imagine Ryley has probably thrown them out. I know I would've since there's no sentimental value in your gym necessities.

The gym is busy, mostly with sailors, but I don't know

them and they don't know me. I've never felt as alone as I do right now, sitting on this weight bench and looking around for someone to work out with. Just as girls go to the bathroom together, guys like to have a gym buddy. We need to spot for each other, hold the punching bag and just be that angry voice that pushes you harder.

River would've been my first choice, but this morning when I came out of my room it was clear that he and Frannie were in the middle of something. I left as soon as I could, with nowhere to go. I can't see Ryley right now. I'm angry with her and am afraid of what might come out of my mouth. It's a hard pill to swallow, walking away from the one person you thought you'd spend the rest of your life with. I guess, in a way, that's what I did. She moved on and that's something I have to accept.

Wandering over to the punching bag, there's a box of gloves beside it that anyone can use. The smart thing to do is find someone to hold my bag and help me lace up, but I don't have time for that. What's building inside me needs to come out and if I don't find a healthy way to expel this aggression, some drunk ass is going to end up being my victim.

Squaring my hips, I jab at the bag. My punch is weak and off center. I don't have the focus I need so I remind myself that I'm a warrior. I'm not allowed to be weak. I jab again, throwing a 1-2-1 combo. My knuckles sting as they come in contact with the bag and I love it.

I need more.

I see his face. I see the look in his eyes as I stare him down. They're black and soulless and the 1-2-3-2 combo doesn't faze him. In my mind he swings. He's weak, a predator. I'm here to stop him. To break him. I sidestep his attempt and land a solid hit to his gut. He bends over, groaning like the piece of shit man that he is. With an uppercut to his nose, blood splatters everywhere and the crunch of cartilage spurs me on. I grab a fistful of his hair in my hand and jam my pistol into his forehead. He begs for mercy, just like those children he was selling on the black market had begged to go home to their moms and dads. I have no mercy for scum like him. He's the reason I'm not home with my family right now.

The loud bang of weights being dropped jars me. My vision is fuzzy. The bright overhead lights are causing me to blink. The bag is swaying back and forth from the pummeling I was giving it. Looking around the gym, people are staring and I can only imagine what they saw.

"You okay, man?"

The voice behind me is that of Tucker McCoy. I sigh in relief that it's him and not the gym's owner. McCoy throws a towel at me and when I bring my hand up to catch it, my red skinned, cracked knuckles stare back at me.

"Shit," I say as I toss the towel over my head.

"Who the fuck are you trying to kill?"

He knows because he was there. I shake my head and sit down on the bench. "I was thinking about Nate when I started, but Renato's face… I don't know, it's been years since I put a bullet in his head. I'm not sure why I'm thinking about him now."

Tacito Renato was the reason we were sent into the jungles of Cuba searching for Senator Christina Charlotte's daughter who had been kidnapped. Charlotte was on the Vice Presidential ticket and didn't want the press involved which blew my mind. Instead she called in a favor to her father-in-law, Brigadier General Chesley, and away we went. We had the child in our custody within days of arriving, but uncovered a sinister child sex ring. Each time we thought we were done, we had orders from the CO sending us back out. There was always something more. The amount of children who had been kidnapped astounded me, and yet no one knew about them. The children were from other countries and of different ages, being hidden in the jungles and sold on the streets for prostitution. For every mastermind we took down, another would take his place within days.

"I started hitting the bag and his face just popped up." Pulling the towel from around my neck, I use it to dab up the blood on my knuckles. "Anyway, what's up?"

"I had a lead on Penny but it didn't pan out. I've lost hope of ever seeing them again."

"Have you spoken with Carole or base housing?"

McCoy takes the seat next to me and sighs. He looks exhausted, and not from fighting an enemy but from fighting the battle going on inside his head. I thought I had it bad with Ryley being engaged to my brother, but to come home and find your wife and child gone is unthinkable.

"Base housing says she left and didn't leave a forwarding address. The private investigator has nothing. The day she left, the CHP's traffic cams were malfunctioning so there's no footage of her on the highway. He says no one matching Claire's description is in any public schools either. Thing is, if she left right after we did, where did the photos come from?"

That seems to be the million-dollar question. Someone here knew we were alive. They stalked our families and used that intel to write us letters. They photographed our kids, wives and parents, and sent them to us. Whoever did this is a sick fuck that needs to be burnt at the stake.

"Someone has the answer," I say, mostly for my own benefit. He knows this. Rask knows this. I want to believe that River knows as well. And no one is going to figure this shit out for us except us. The problem is, our access is limited and people on base already consider us an enigma.

"I just want to know if they're okay," he says. "If Penny wants a divorce, I'd give it to her, but I have this gut feeling that they're hurt and in danger. Penny isn't resilient. She didn't grow up in the military like Ryley did. I need to find them, Arch. I have to know they're okay."

If it were Ryley and EJ that were missing, I'd be moving heaven and earth to find them. I wouldn't care who stood in my way. But when the trail runs cold, you're at a standstill and you don't know where to look next.

"I think we need to pay Carole a visit. Besides, I haven't seen her in a couple of weeks and she missed my party."

Today is my first day back on base. It feels both welcoming and odd at the same time. Sailors and other service people mill around as if nothing is wrong. As if the two guys walking into the JAG office haven't been dead for six years. I didn't want to come back here even though I'm still enlisted. I guess maybe I'm waiting for a formal apology, but I know it's never coming. Since our return the Navy hasn't reached out to us. You'd think, under the circumstances, they'd want us all on base until their extensive debriefing was concluded. To date we haven't been asked one question. We haven't opened the door to an NCIS agent.

It's as if no one cares.

Walking into the JAG office, McCoy and I stand side-by-side. I have to admit that it's nice having a Staff Judge Advocate at your disposal. The receptionist makes eye contact with us, but makes no attempt to move or greet us. It doesn't escape my notice that she presses a button on her phone before asking if she can help us.

"Is this where I'll find Commander Clarke?" I ask because it's been years since I've been here and a lot of things have changed.

"Yes, it is."

"I'd like to see her please," I tell her. She looks down at her phone, shaking her head.

"I'm sorry but Commander Clarke is unavailable."

McCoy groans next to me. We're both eager for help and Carole is the only one I know that can guide us in the right direction. I'm not expecting her to get me the answers, but she'll know where to send us.

"Do you know when Commander Clarke will return?"

"No, I don't." Her tone is flippant and dismissive. In my many years of being a SEAL, one thing you learn is how to read people. Her posture, tone and overall attitude tells me that she doesn't want us here... that we're not *allowed* here.

With my hands spread wide along the edge of the counter, I lean forward. "Do not mistake me for a stupid man. I need to see Commander Clarke and it's urgent. Now where can I find her or when will she be back?"

"I'm right here, Evan."

Carole appears in the doorway with files in her arms. My eyes travel from her to the receptionist and back again, hoping to communicate that she's been an issue.

"Sabrina, as with any other lawyer in this building, if our family members need to see us, you call. And I know you're well aware of who this man is."

"My apologies, Commander Clarke," she says as she falls into her seat and sure as shit, her hand slides over to her phone, pressing another button.

"Follow me," Carole tells us as she turns down the hallway she appeared from. McCoy and I follow her, passing numerous offices until we turn into the same one as Carole. She waits, shutting the door behind us after we step into her office.

"You're dressed like a civilian today," I say, pointing out the obvious.

"I was having lunch with your brother earlier," she says, pointing at the seats in front of her desk for us to sit down in. "I'm happy you're here though, I want to ask you some questions."

I try not to let the fact that she's already met with Nate bother me. My jaw ticks from anger and frustration. Why is it that everywhere I turn, there he is? This isn't his fight. It's mine.

"Who gave you your orders?"

"Ma'am?" McCoy says. I don't know about him, but the answer seems obvious to me.

"Captain O'Keefe," I say, knowing that she knows this answer. My training tells me that I should ask one back, but I want to know where she's going with this.

"Do you know this for a fact?"

I look from her to McCoy and both of us shake our heads. Carole slides a piece of paper toward us and we lean forward to read it. It's our orders, telling us the where, why and what of the operation. The only thing questionable is the space where O'Keefe's signature should be at the bottom. It's not there.

"I don't understand," McCoy says.

Carole takes the paper back and places it in her briefcase, along with the file that she pulled it from. "I'm doing what I can to figure this out, but Evan, I want you to talk to Nate. He wants to help and he's been doing his own digging. Right now, he has a little more freedom on base. Keep your eyes and ears open and your mouths shut. Do not talk to anyone about this except for me. I'll be at Ryley's tonight. I think you guys should join us."

There's a brief knock on the door before it opens. When Carole stands, McCoy and I both turn to find the Commander of the Southwest Region in her doorway. We stand to attention, but he ignores us.

"Just stopping in to say 'hi' and introduce myself. I'm Admiral Jonah Ingram." He stands there, staring at us before closing the door. McCoy and I both exhale and look at each other before we sit down. I grip the arm rests as my mind starts running every scenario possible.

"Why's he here?" McCoy is brave enough to ask, but I want to know why he didn't talk to us, ask for a meeting. Is the Commander of Navy, Southwest Region not concerned that four of his men are alive and well instead of buried six feet under?

She sits calmly, but all the color has drained from her face. "Captain O'Keefe hasn't returned to base since you guys arrived home. A body was found the day Nate returned but is now missing from the morgue. Now I don't know about you, but if four SEALs return from the dead and their Captain disappears, all sorts of red flags are flying. Yet, there hasn't been a single news crew or reporter around and people are acting odd. No one seems to care about any of this."

"But ma'am, this is San Diego," McCoy states. "Dead bodies are a daily occurrence."

"You're right, unless you're me and looking for answers as to why my son-in-law and his team disappeared for six years." Carole folds her hands together and sighs. "I know I look for cause in everything, but before you left, Senator Lawson was hanging around the base. I know you don't know who he is –"

"Wait, I've heard that name… Rick, he said it. The guy is from Florida or something like that. Rick says he was here about a month before we left and he hadn't seen him again until a few weeks ago. What does he have to do with this?"

"Ingram is Lawson's father and while it may just be coincidence, I don't like it. Things aren't adding up – and why would the Commander be here?" Carole asks, as she stands and starts to pace.

"Nothing has been adding up since we deployed," McCoy states, earning an ominous look from Carole. River has even stated that our orders seemed a bit out of place, but we didn't question them.

I think it's time we start.

chapter 19
Nate

THERE HASN'T BEEN A TIME in the past six years that I haven't jumped when Ryley has called, until today. As much as I want to sit down and talk with Evan, spending the afternoon with him is not high on my list right now, especially with his team members and Jensen and Carole around. Jensen has never been shy about his feelings toward me. Evan was, and probably still is, the son he's always wanted. At best, he tolerates me because he has to. But now that Evan is back, I can't imagine Jensen wants to pay attention to me at all. If that's not going to be awkward, I don't know what is.

I walk to the back gate instead of through the house. I don't know why, but with Evan here, it feels like I shouldn't. After giving Ryley the letter that Evan wrote, I've been second-guessing my spot in Ryley's life. Maybe it was my subconscious that forgot about the letter. It had been so long since he gave it to me that I just didn't remember it until yesterday. I knew that as soon as I handed it to her, I'd be sealing my own fate. He was madly in love with her at eighteen. I can only imagine what that letter says.

Steeling myself for what's surely going to be a rocky afternoon, I open the gate and walk into the backyard. Deefur is the first one to greet me. At least *he's* happy to see me. One can always count on man's best friend. Ryley walks over to me and I pause. I can be like Evan and take her here, piss on her leg and show him that she's mine or I can treat her like I've always treated her - with respect.

The respect always wins out where I'm concerned and I kiss her lightly on the cheek. "These are for you," I tell her, showing her the flowers I'm holding. Her hand caresses mine as she grabs a hold of the packaged stems. Her eyes never leave mine as she inhales the flowers' fragrant scent.

"They're beautiful."

"Not nearly as beautiful as you," I say and this time I ignore the people in the backyard and pull her into a kiss. When she pulls away there's a smile where my lips just were.

"I'm going to go put these in water." She's gone before I can respond and even though her family and mine are mingling in the backyard, I feel utterly alone. Jensen and Evan are deep in conversation, and it makes me wonder whether my showmanship was even witnessed. Did Evan see Ryley react to me? Did he see how good Ryley and I are together? And then there's my sister, hanging on every word coming out of Evan's mouth right now, laughing at anything he says. Where's my greeting? And more importantly, where's my son?

Climbing the steps of the deck, I step into the house. Ryley is standing at the sink with her attention focused on the backyard. I want to be in her head right now. I want to know what she's thinking. I want to know where we stand because we're supposed to be getting married and she's still wearing my ring.

I place my hand on the counter and press my chest against her back. Whispering against her neck, I say, "Penny for your thoughts?"

"Is that all I'm worth to you, a penny?" she laughs softly and leans into me. "Do you remember when everything was simple?"

I sigh and sag against her. "Do you mean before I left on this last mission?"

Ryley shakes her head. "Before, like when we were teenagers and it was spring. Do you remember that day it rained —"

"We lived in Washington, Ry, it rained all the time." She turns in my arms, her face full of excitement.

"That day we all went to the beach and it started raining. We were covered in sand and Evan was freaking out because your mom had told us 'no sand in the car'. You started snapping us with the towel to get the sand off not realizing that the wet towel, mixed with cold air and sand, was leaving welts on everyone."

"My dad was pissed when he got calls from all the other parents."

"I want to go back to those days where everything was simple."

"We can't," I say as I pull her into a hug. "There's so much I'd love to change, but we can't." When she pulls away there are tears in her eyes.

"Let's change the one thing we have control over. You know I love you and want us to be a family. We talked about getting married and I know you asked for space, but you're still wearing my ring. Call me stupid, but that gives me a ton of hope."

Ryley shakes her head as her tears fall. "I can't, Nate. Not yet."

"I know," I say as I cup her cheek. "It was stupid of me to ask, but I had to because I made a promise to you that I'd take care of you and I'd never lie to you." Taking a deep breath, I ready myself for what I'm about to say. "I've received my orders, and I'm set to leave at the end of next week. I can't leave knowing things are up in the air with us."

Ryley looks down at her hand before her tear-stained eyes meet mine. "You can't leave. You have to tell them no, or tell them that your brother is home and it's just not possible. Evan left and didn't come back... you can't leave me. Not now."

I pull her back into my arms to curb the panic attack. I should've known this would be the result. It was never going to be easy telling her that I was leaving, but it's not like I can keep it a secret.

"Nate, promise me that you won't leave."

"Ry —"

"No, promise me," she demands, pulling away from me. "Evan just got back. You both need to repair your relationship and call me crazy and paranoid, but if you leave, what guarantees do I have that you'll come back?"

"There's a war —"

"NO!" she roars, pushing me away. "You don't leave. You tell whomever you need to that you can't go on this deployment. You tell them that you don't trust them." Ryley wipes angrily at her tears, smudging her make-up. "You tell them that your family comes first and you're staying here to find out what happened to your brother."

"Ryley?" her head turns at the sound of both Carole and Evan saying her name.

"You're leaving?" this time the question is directed at me from Livvie.

"It's my job," I tell her and anyone else listening.

"It was Evan's job and look at what happened to him. Who's to say that the same won't happen to you?"

"Tink, don't," Evan says to her. I'm not sure if he's defending me right now or not.

Livvie stands next to Ryley, both women in my life staring me down with their arms crossed over their chests. In a normal situation I'd look to Evan for guidance, but with me out of the picture he has a clear shot at Ryley. Right now it feels like I'm facing a firing squad and it's not going to matter what I say or do.

"Mom, can't you do something?"

"Ryley," I say, getting her attention. "Your mom has no say in the orders we get, you know that. Short of breaking my leg, you know there's nothing that can be done."

"I could break your leg. Oddly enough, I'd get a perverse satisfaction by doing so." I wish to hell I could say Evan is joking, but he's not.

"Thanks, Evan, but I think I'm okay." He shrugs, as if it's no big deal that he just offered to break my leg.

We're all in a standoff. Ryley and Livvie are on one side of the kitchen with Carole and Jensen on the other. Jenson hasn't said much, not that I thought he would, but it would be nice for some support. Evan and I are in the middle of this. We're the tug-of-war. Both of us are being pushed and pulled in every direction but the one we both want to be heading in.

The sound of an abrupt knock on the door startles us, even causes me to jump. Deefur barks and EJ's thundering footsteps are heard coming down the stairs.

"I get it," he yells, just as Evan and I make a move for the door.

"I'll get it," Jensen says loudly as he brushes by me. Ryley uses the break to her advantage and starts pulling food out of the refrigerator. Livvie and her mom start to help while Evan and I stand in the kitchen like statues. It's a face off - or a childish stare off - like EJ and I sometimes have over a bowl of ice cream.

EJ comes running into the kitchen and tackles me. I pick him up, and ignore the disgruntled sounds that Evan is making.

"I didn't know yous was here." At what point in a parent's life do you start to correct your child's speech? I know that when he gets to school everything will change. Those days are something I'm not looking forward to.

"I just got here. I was about to go on a secret mission to find you."

"I'll go hide," he says as he squirms out of my arms and runs off, barely missing Jensen who is standing in the doorway. His face is white as can be.

"What's wrong?" Evan has the foresight to ask before I can utter the same question.

Jensen looks at us and down at the paper he's holding. His steps into the kitchen are cautious and he holds the paper as if it's fragile. Setting it down on the kitchen island, he stands there shaking his head.

"I don't know what you guys are doing, but you need to stop," his words are monotone and they send chills down my spine. Evan, Carole and I all step forward and look at what he set down.

STOP
OR
SHE DIES

The words are cut out from a magazine and arranged like a ransom note. Ryley steps forward and I wish I could've caught her before she saw the paper. The bowl she's holding slips from her hands and crashes to the ground. The sound of shattering porcelain echoes throughout the room. Her hand covers her mouth and somewhere from within a scream emerges.

It's Evan who catches her before she falls. I'm grateful, but also jealous. She's mine and I should be the one to comfort her.

"What did you do?" Jensen asks as he looks from me, to Carole and then Evan. "Why is someone leaving death threats for my daughter on her porch?"

"I've been digging –'

"I've been asking –'

"I've been looking—'

The three of us say at once causing Jensen's head to turn.

"Tink, go upstairs with EJ, please." Evan asks because he knows she'll do whatever he says. It doesn't escape my notice that she has tears in her eyes. She knows the magnitude of what's happening and what that note means. Evan's return and our subsequent investigation has rattled someone and it's someone close to us. Now, the question is who?

"Outside," Carole demands. You would think after her daughter's life has just been threatened that she'd be more upset, but she's calm on the outside. We follow her out to

138

the backyard for reasons unknown to me. "Gather around, and listen closely," she says. "The three of us have been digging and the more I find hidden, the more I'm convinced something transpired that the Navy doesn't want us to know about. I don't want any of you talking about this in the house, am I clear?"

"Carole —"

"No, listen to me Jensen. I know I'm a conspiracy theorist, but my gut is telling me that I'm right on this one. Four highly trained and decorated SEALs do *not* go into the jungle and just disappear. They don't receive care packages and updates from home after their loved ones have buried their bodies. And if I wasn't right, we wouldn't receive a death threat on the one-day that we're all at the same house. Who knew you guys were coming here today?"

"McCoy, but you invited him… and Frannie. I told her when I was leaving that I'd be back later. She asked where I was going and I told her."

Carole nods and looks at me. "No one but Carter and Lois would assume I'm over here if I'm not at their house."

"McCoy isn't in the right frame of mind to do this. He's hurting, just like you guys. But Frannie —"

"Hold up, Mom. You think *Frannie* has something to do with this?"

"I didn't say that but tell me this Ryley, who was with you the whole time Evan was gone?"

Ryley steps back and looks at me. "Aside from you and Dad - Nate, Frannie, Carter and Lois," she says as her eyes go wide. "That could mean that —"

"Carter wouldn't," I say and am shocked to find Evan nodding in agreement.

"People do the unthinkable when they find themselves stuck in certain situations. We have to find out what that situation is, what was the catalyst that set this in motion. Someone knows something," Carole says pleadingly. "Jensen, I know you're worried about Ryley and EJ, I am too, but she has two highly lethal men in her life that will kill before they let a hair on either of their heads be harmed. They'll protect her."

"What about you?" he asks.

"I'll be safe," she says to Jensen.

Carole is right, regardless of whom Ryley and EJ belong to right now, Evan and I won't let anything happen to her. Same goes for Carole.

chapter 20
Evan

IT'S OFFICIAL... A FIVE-YEAR-OLD HAS more logic than I do. When did that happen? After a tension filled dinner, Jensen suggested that one of us start staying with Ryley. An argument ensued and I lost simply because EJ asked that his dad spend the night. I didn't think tonight was the time to assert my position in his life, and as much as I wanted to pound my chest and go all Tarzan on everyone, I can't compete with the imploring looks from EJ. Ryley says that I'll learn, but right now I don't want to. I want to give in to every little request he has and give him the world. I want to learn what makes that little boy tick, what his favorite cereal is and whether he puts ketchup on his eggs like I do.

When I look at him I see me.

When he looks at me I want him to see his dad.

"Tough night?" Rick asks as he wipes down the bar. Magoo's is empty for the most part. There's a couple in the corner, but they're so into each other they're not paying attention to anyone else.

"You could say that."

"I'd ask you what's bothering ya, but I can probably figure it out."

I finish off the beer in my mug and slide it toward him. "I imagine that you've heard a lot of stories, people tell you a lot of things. So let me ask you, have you ever heard of anyone going through what we did?"

Rick takes my mug and refills it, placing it on the bar along with a fresh bowl of popcorn and nuts. I shouldn't be hungry but can honestly say I didn't eat a thing at Ryley's earlier, so bar food it is.

When Jensen showed us that note I wanted to lose my shit, but figured that's what the people who are doing this want. It seems like they want the fight but aren't willing to show face. They're hiding behind death threats being left on front porches. Cowards... that's what they are.

"I hear things," Rick says, leaning closer to me. "I'm told things. And some people aren't careful with how loud they are. Take that couple behind you." I turn, looking quickly. "He's having an affair, but his lady there doesn't know it. He came in last night with a different woman."

"That's stupid."

"Mhm, but what's worse is that he came in at lunch with his friends, bragging about it."

Some men don't get it. I'd give anything to have Ryley in my arms, and here's this man cheating on his partner. He makes me want to go over to him and bash some sense into him.

"Ever hear anything about me or my team?"

"You know you always wonder if you missed something. I like to think I'm fairly observant, like that reporter chick. She spends a lot of time in here looking for you, but you're never in here at the same time. Then there's that Senator dude. I don't like him. He sits in the corner on his phone and always orders a beer that he doesn't touch. Never talks to anyone, never meets with anyone."

"What else do you know about this Lawson guy?"

Rick shrugs, leaving to help someone at the bar. I turn around and look at the couple in the corner. I feel sorry for the woman. She's all over him, completely smitten and he's just sitting there. He wants the attention, but isn't willing to give it back to her. He looks tired, likely realizing that cheating is hard work. Keeping your stories straight takes a lot of effort.

The idea of them disgusts me and I realize that could've been me. I was pushing Ryley to be with me knowing full well that she belonged to another. I didn't care if she compromised her relationship with Nate because as far as I was concerned – and still am – he took her from me.

A suit walks in, his eyes glued to his cell phone as he sits down in the corner. The door opens again and in walks a woman. I look away from her and back to the man in the corner. He doesn't check his surroundings and definitely doesn't look up when the lady walks by.

Turning back around, I take a handful of popcorn. This is as good as it gets for me tonight. Going back to River's doesn't appeal to me. After Carole asked who knew we'd be at Ryley's tonight, the thought of seeing Frannie turns my stomach. I can't fathom that she'd have something to do with this mess, but part of me wonders. She was ready for River to come home. That right there is a red flag for me.

The thought of Nate in the house with Ryley after EJ goes to bed makes my blood boil. I'm happy that someone is there with her, but it should be me. Picking up my mug, I down the tepid beer and signal for another one. From here, I can walk if I need to. Or Rick will call me a cab. In fact, the less I remember about tonight the better.

"Do you always sit at the bar alone?"

"Thanks," I say to Rick after he puts my fresh beer down, ignoring the question that's just been asked. I know the polite thing to do is acknowledge the woman next to me, but I have no desire to get to know anyone and I don't want to give her a false hope for the night.

"Not alone, I have my friend Rick here." It's really the only thing I can say, aside from "I'm not interested".

Rick looks from me to her before he leaves us alone. I'm going to have to remind him that my heart belongs to Ryley until she chooses Nate. It'll probably still be hers until I can figure out how to move on. That's not something I like thinking about though. Each morning I wake up with a small bit of hope. However, after the afternoon at the park, I told her I was walking away. For all I know I just handed her right over to Nate. Maybe if I grow a set, I'll ask her about their relationship tomorrow.

But then again, maybe not. I've had enough heartache to last me a lifetime.

"I have something for you."

I try not to roll my eyes at her come on, but the lack of effort is futile.

"Not interested," I finally say, hoping she gets the hint.

"Oh, I think you are," she replies, and I finally give in and look at her. Big mistake.

Her caramel colored eyes are mysterious. Her brown hair has blonde highlights and is styled perfectly, shaping her face. A face I know and remember well. She's changed. She's more sophisticated than the last time I saw her.

"Well, if I knew it was you, I would've pulled the stool out for you."

"It's good to see you, Evan."

"You too, Cara." I start to lean over to hug her, but she shakes her head discretely.

"The man in the corner; I'm tailing him. We need to make this look like we're flirting."

Peering over my shoulder quickly, I see the man who walked in earlier. It dawns on me that this guy is Lawson, the guy Rick has been talking about.

"You're the reporter?"

She nods, and thanks Rick for the wine he's set down for her. "I am." I can't tell if she's lying or if she's a legit reporter. The last time I saw her she was just starting out at the CIA. Because we were together for family functions, Ryley and I were interviewed and asked a lot of invasive questions. It was all worth it once Cara told us she got the job.

"You've asked about me?"

Cara takes a sip of her wine before answering. "We're interested in what went down in Cuba. Call it an unhealthy curiosity or a hazard of the job. Either way there are things we'd like to know and asking is sometimes the easiest way to find out."

"We?" I question, hoping that she gives me the answer I seek. Is she truly a reporter now or is she undercover?

Cara smiles shyly and touches my arm. I'm thankful it's for show. Cara's an attractive woman, but she doesn't flip my switch. "We… work. You know."

"So that hasn't changed. You're still doing the bidding for the Navy? Gathering information for the big dogs? Pretending to hide in corners?"

She laughs, hopefully remembering that we used to joke about everything we thought the spooks did.

Cara sighs. "A lot changed when you died. I left for Virginia. I got my dream, but I recently switched to the sprawling city of DC," she says.

I'm a bit shocked and give her a sideways glance. She cracks a small smile. Last I knew she wanted nothing to do with bringing people down, she just wanted to spy on them. "Feds?"

"Yeah."

"Am I in trouble?"

Cara shakes her head. "No, but you took out a heavy hitter and lived to tell about it. That's why I'm here."

"I'm not sure you can call this living, Cara. I came home to a family that had moved on without me. I have a son who knows I'm his dad but doesn't want to call me dad. My fiancée… I'm assuming you know what happened there."

Cara shakes her head. "I left Nate. He didn't leave me for Ryley if that's what you're asking."

"I wasn't, but thanks for clearing that up."

She smiles, bringing her glass to her lips. I think I've struck a nerve because she lingers. She's taking her time with the wine and her next question. Or maybe it's my turn to ask something.

"What did you mean by 'heavy hitter'?"

"Tacito Renato was a major player in the sex ring you guys busted up, only you were supposed to capture him. We wanted to interrogate him, get him to turn on the others, but you put a bullet between his eyes instead."

"He was raping a little girl about six years old. He's lucky that's all I did," I say, as I slam my mug down on the counter. Rick is there to clean up my mess, making me feel like shit for spilling my beer.

"He's not the only one," Cara says as nonchalantly as possible.

"What are you talking about?"

"My tail. We believe the Senator is into pedophilia, but I'm having a hard time proving it. One day we see it on his computer and the next it's wiped clean. I've been following him for a year or so. He'll go into strip clubs, watch the show and then go home or to his hotel. He disguises himself so he doesn't get caught. I want to arrest him, but I'm not ready yet."

To say I'm confused is an understatement. This senator is Ingram's son that no one seems to know about and he's a closet perv who may or may not be into some fucked up shit.

"What does this have to do with me or my Team?"

"Just you," she says, turning to face me. "Renato and Lawson were friends and I have a feeling he's here to find out from you what Renato confessed to before you shut his lights out."

"He didn't say jack shit, didn't even plead for his life." It's not entirely true, but he never mentioned Lawson's name. I know it's been years, but I would've remembered that much. "Cara, why are you here?"

"I go where he goes until I have enough for an arrest warrant. When we started digging, I saw your name. I was there when you...when everything went down... so it was a bit of a shock."

"What do you mean you saw my name?"

"I have every reason to believe Lawson knew you guys were alive. An email he wrote to someone that goes by the initials JI asked what would happen to him when the four come home."

"And you think that's about my Team?"

"I do, now I just have to figure out who JI is."

"Admiral Jonah Ingram is my guess. He's the Commander, Southwest Region and he showed up on base today." I look over my shoulder at Lawson. His head is down and he's typing away on his phone. "Ingram is his father according to Carole."

If I didn't believe that my life was screwed up already, I do now.

chapter 21
Nate

I DON'T KNOW HOW LONG I've been watching Ryley. I'm not even sure she knows I'm behind her. But here I am standing in the doorway to EJ's room spying on the woman I want to marry while she stares at all the photos of my brother which cover the wall. I wouldn't think her being in here is odd except for the fact that EJ spent the night with me in the guest room.

I should be jealous, but I'm not. This isn't the first time I've found her like this and I can only imagine how many nights she's spent in here since Evan returned. When Lois came up with the idea to wallpaper EJ's room with photos of Evan, I thought it was great. I even spent time in here, talking to him and EJ, reliving our childhood as I told his son stories.

When EJ was born, Ryley had every intention of telling EJ that Evan was his father. But then daycare happened and when I was home, I'd pick him up because I needed to feel close to Evan. However, children are smart and they follow what their peers do so when EJ saw his little friends getting picked up by their dads, he started calling me "Dad". At first, I was against it. I didn't want to dishonor my brother's memory. But on the other hand, I didn't want my nephew growing up without a father and I honestly couldn't see Ryley with anyone else.

Cara didn't like it, and I understood why. She loved EJ, but didn't want him calling me "Dad". I should've respected her request when she asked that only our children refer to me as that, but I didn't. I couldn't look my nephew in the eyes, the same eyes that I felt held my brother's soul, and tell him no. I still can't. It's not what tore Cara and me apart. Ryley isn't either. Life is. But it's also the same life that has given me the opportunity to be EJ's dad and a partner to Ryley. It's the same life that I'm fighting to keep.

"What are you doing?" I whisper to Ryley as I enter EJ's room. She smiles softly, but doesn't answer. Her being in here doesn't require an answer anyway. I know why she's in here. It's still early and the sun is barely peaking over the horizon. EJ's window is open and there's a cool ocean breeze coming in. It's mornings like this that I'm thankful Evan had the good sense to use his inheritance from our dad to buy a house near the ocean.

Standing against the wall, I slide down until my butt is firmly on the ground. Pulling my knees up, I rest my arms on top of them. Maybe the wall of Evan has all the answers, but then again, maybe it doesn't.

"Do you sit in here a lot when I'm not home?"

"I used to, but you helped me heal. If it weren't for you, I'd be a shell of the woman I am today."

"EJ did that for you, Ry. You're strong because of him."

Ryley wipes the tears from her eyes and I fight the urge

to pull her from her chair and into my lap. It took so long for us both to heal and find a happy medium. We both lost a lot in the last six years, but we gained a lot as well. Evan was taken from us, but our family was blessed by the arrival of EJ who was my last connection to my brother. Then I lost Cara to my own selfishness and my inability to see what was good for her... good for *us*. All Cara wanted to do was love me and I wouldn't allow her to.

"Do you ever wonder how things should've been?"

"Every day," she says in a voice barely above a whisper. Ryley repositions herself, pulling her blanket a little higher. It's not cold in here, but I imagine the security of having herself covered is what she needs right now.

"You and Evan would be married," I say, even though it's not reality.

"And probably barefoot and pregnant again," she says with a hint of laughter. "He once said in a letter that he wants to have his own football team and it didn't matter if we had nothing but girls because girls could play too." Ryley pauses as she plays with the corner of her blanket. "Do you ever wonder about Cara?"

"Cara couldn't accept me for me." I know why Cara asked me not to re-enlist. It made sense then and still makes sense now, but to me, I'm a SEAL and I'll always be one.

"Right after Evan died, Lois took me to a grief meeting. You know the type, where we sit around in a circle and tell everyone our story. Anyway, this woman told everyone that she lost her sister and brother-in-law, but that her sister was still alive. The counselor asked her to explain what she meant and she said that she and her sister had both married soldiers, but hers came back and now her sister wouldn't speak to her anymore. That's how I see Cara. She was here when Evan died and saw what it did to us. She didn't want to experience that. No one does, really.

"Being with a SEAL is hard. You're gone a lot. There are times when you don't make it home for dinner. There are days when we can't talk because you're off training someplace. There's an unknown and I can understand why she was hesitant."

"It's in the past now, Ryley. Besides, everyone is going to feel differently," I say, as I rub my hand up and down her calf.

"I hate the word 'feel'," she scoffs. "I'm not sure how I'm *supposed* to feel, Nate. I'm so torn in half that I can't even breathe. I asked you both for space and you've given it to me, but it's not helping. I need you both in my life and I know it's not possible. I want to walk in my front door and have you both sitting on the couch waiting. It's sick and twisted, but it's what I want. I want my cake with the frosting and side of ice cream and I want to eat it in my bed.

"If I choose Evan, it hurts you and you're my best friend. You're my rock, my foundation. Choosing Evan damages your relationship with EJ and confuses him. I know that's on me. I know EJ's pain will be my burden to bear. But if I choose you, I've lost Evan again and I'm not sure I can survive that. It's selfish and I hate myself for thinking that way. But as I sit here and stare at him on the wall and think about everything he's missed because someone in this world chose to take him away from us, I ask myself how I can do that? How can I deny him something that he didn't give up willingly?"

This time when she sobs I'm there to pull her into my arms. Her tears soak my bare skin as she muffles her cries in my neck. I knew this moment was coming, I just didn't expect it to be today.

"I want to take your pain away. I do. I'd give anything for us to go back two months ago and make time stop. You're a good woman and you don't deserve this."

"That's just it. I don't want time to stop. I want Evan here. And because I'm having those feelings while engaged to another man, I *do* deserve this. The letter 'A' should be branded into my skin because of the thoughts and feelings I'm having for another man."

"Ryley, we've been dealt the shittiest hand in Vegas. I can't beg and plead for you to stay with me. I wouldn't do that. I know how you feel about Evan. I've witnessed it. I watched it grow from a simple romance to something powerful and unwavering. I know you and I aren't on that level and I never expected us to be, but you know that I love you. You know that you're my world and I'd do anything for you, even step aside if that was what you wanted."

Ryley doesn't say anything and that scares me. Did I just willingly hand her over to Evan without meaning to do so? I want to think that I didn't, but I'm honestly not so sure. It's hard to compete with someone, but it's even harder to compete with your twin. Our family has been divided since he passed away. My mother tried to destroy Ryley, and I stepped in to protect her just as I said I would. I didn't count on falling in love with her, though. This is more than an old high school crush. At least it is for me.

We sit on the floor until EJ comes in looking for us. He crawls into my awaiting arm and snuggles into his mom and me. This is a moment that I need to preserve forever because my time could be up very soon. I could walk out of here today and never see them again. It'd kill me, but if Ryley asked me to do that, I would.

"What are you guys doing?" Livvie stands in the doorway, hair piled on top of her head and half asleep.

"Just hanging out," I tell her.

"Uh huh, well come on EJ, let's go make some breakfast."

"And toon toons," he says as he chases her out of the room.

"I'm going to go shower." Ryley disengages herself from my arms and even though it's warm in here, I instantly feel cold. I know I have to do something to save us, but I'm not sure what.

"Want to go on a date?" I blurt out, without a plan. "We haven't been out in a while, obviously, and we could use a night out."

"I'd like that." Her smile says everything and nothing at the same time. She stands, leaving me on the floor alone. No kiss goodbye, just a smile. I'm not sure how I'm supposed to take that.

"Can I take EJ to the zoo?" Ryley looks up at me before answering Livvie. We've been relaxing on the couch for the past hour or so, just watching TV and pretending like our world is perfect.

EJ is standing next to Livvie with his hands bent like dog paws, his way of begging. "I don't see why not. Do you need any money?"

"No, I'm all set. We'll be back by dinner." EJ jumps up

with a triumphant "Yes!" and doesn't even say goodbye to us. As soon as the door shuts, Ryley is back in my arms, cuddled up where she belongs.

The doorbell rings and Deefur starts barking. He runs to the door before I have a chance to get up and answer it.

"Can't believe they forgot something," she says as I follow behind the anxious dog.

"What'd you forget?" I say, swinging the door open.

"Hello, little brother."

Evan stands before me with a cocky grin on his face. Behind him stands the woman who left me and has been on my mind all day. Call it fate, or just dumb luck, either way I'm not sure how I feel about seeing her right now.

"Cara," I say, sounding out of breath. I want to ask Evan if he called her, brought her for a reason, but I know he didn't. He wouldn't have known how to find her.

"Hello, Nate." She's formal, and not how I remember her at all. The way she used to say my name told me that she cared and right now she makes me sound like a subject.

"Are you going to invite us in?"

I want him to leave and take Cara with him, but I don't say that. Instead I push the door open and step aside. Evan walks in first and as soon as Cara is over the threshold, I shut the door behind her.

"How long have you lived here?"

This is why I don't want Cara here. I don't want to do this with her. Answering twenty questions about my relationship with Ryley that started well after she and I broke up is none of her business. But in her line of work, she probably already knows how long I've lived here.

"What are you doing here, Cara?"

155

She turns and smiles softly. "I think we have a mutual acquaintance." She leaves me standing there as she walks into the living room.

"Cara," I hear excitement in Ryley's voice, and when I round the corner they're hugging. I guess that's a good sign.

"I knew you'd play dirty, but this is low," I say to Evan as quietly as I can.

He chuckles. "Cara found me," he says as his facial expression changes. "She has information that I think you'll be interested in."

I watch her and Ryley talk animatedly on the couch, wondering what Cara could know and if any of it will help us figure out this mess.

"But, yeah it's pretty damn convenient, isn't it?" he says with a smirk on his face.

chapter 22
Evan

BRINGING CARA HERE IS PROBABLY the best idea I've ever had. Seeing Nate's reaction to his ex-girlfriend standing next to me was priceless, except that wasn't my intent. She's here strictly for work. The simple fact that she's willing to help us means a lot and I'm not willing to pass up the resources she has. I'm not telling my brother that, though. He can think whatever he wants and if it gets him away from Ryley sooner, so be it.

As much as I want to see Ryley and Cara hate each other, they don't. They're standing in the middle of the living room hugging and carrying on like long lost friends. I don't know how Cara can be like that with her, knowing that Ryley is now engaged to Nate. Maybe it's just me that has a problem with Ryley and Nate.

Not wanting to be caught in another awkward situation, I head into the kitchen. I'm thankful that Nate isn't in here because I need to get my head straight. Cara asked some important questions last night that got me thinking and that's how we ended up here this morning. Carole, McCoy, River and Rask are going to be joining us as well. We need to put our heads together and map out a timeline.

When Ryley walks into the kitchen she finds me leaning up against the counter. We make eye contact and there's a small hint of a smile that's playing on her lips. I want to taste those lips so damn badly, but I told her that I couldn't do this anymore and I meant it. It's not that I don't want her, I do. Those feelings will never go away, but I can't be a yo-yo...

If she wants me she's going to have to show me.

Looking at her now I see the same beautiful woman who sent my heart into a tailspin the first day we met, bruised eye and all. Every fiber of my being is pushing me to go to her. To turn my mind off and listen to my heart, but I can't. Being without her for six years was hard enough, and knowing she was waiting for me when I came home is what kept me going. Right now I feel like I'm dying on the inside without her and I don't know how to tell her how I feel without sounding like a broken record. In all our years together I've only pleaded with her once and that was when she tried to break-up with me before I went to basic training. It may be time to start begging again.

"Did you call Cara? Did you ask her to come... for Nate?" she asks, moving closer to me. I'm not sure if I should be offended that she and Nate think so little of me, but whatever. If Cara being here works to my advantage, so be it.

"I think you give me too much credit, babe. She found me at Magoo's last night." Ryley is close enough to me that if I were to push myself away from the counter I'd be in front of her in a flash. She wouldn't be able to resist me even if she tried.

"We should talk," Cara says as she enters the kitchen with Nate following, interrupting whatever moment Ryley and I were having. His disgruntled appearance doesn't escape my attention either. I'm glad to see that he's feeling like I have this past month, even if Cara is only here to do a job.

"Outside," Nate orders. I motion for Ryley to go first because I like watching her walk in front of me with her stupid short shorts and oversized Navy t-shirt that I have no doubt was mine. I used to buy the shirts and wear them a few times before she'd think she was stealing them. She'll never know I let her do it because there's just something sexy about the woman you love walking around in your clothes.

"Where's EJ?" I ask, as we walk down the deck stairs into the backyard.

"Livvie took him to the zoo," Ryley says as she looks over her shoulder. Everything moves in slow motion as her hair sways and her smile fades when she sees me. "What's wrong?"

I shake my head and stick my hand out. "Can I use your phone?" She reaches into her back pocket and hands it over without hesitation. I pull out the piece of paper I've been keeping phone numbers on and dial Rask's number.

"Hey man, can you head to the zoo and look for my sister? She has my son with her and I just want to make sure they're okay."

"Yeah, sure. Do you want me to hang out with them?"

I think about it but realize that Livvie would probably freak out if she thought they were in any danger and that's the last thing I want. "No, just watch them and make sure they get back to Ryley's okay."

"No problem. You'll fill me in when I get there?" Rask

asks. He's lost too, but differently. When we left for Cuba, he was just a young kid and a year out of BUD/S training. Since our return, his family has disowned him, saying they buried their son. He wants to prove to them that he is who he says he is.

"Yeah, I'll be here. Please, keep them safe." I'm not above begging where my family is concerned.

"You know I will."

Ending my call, I hand Ryley her cell phone back. "I'm almost afraid to ask, but I have to know. Are they okay?"

"They'll be fine," I reassure her, using this opportunity to push her hair behind her ear. I let my fingers linger on her skin, enjoying the jolt of electricity.

"When are you going to get a cell phone, Archer?"

I shrug. "Why, babe, do you want to sext me?"

Ryley's eyes go wide and I laugh. "You'd probably like that."

"Oh Ry, you have no idea." I kiss her quickly on her nose and step aside, leaving her standing there. Thing is, there hasn't ever been a reason for me to believe I would need things like a cell phone or a car. I've been using Ryley's car since I returned, but I'm sure she's ready to have it back. At this point I don't even know what I have for money. I should probably sit down with Ryley or my mom and figure that out so I can re-establish myself in society.

As soon as everyone arrives, we gather around the picnic

table. I remember when Ryley and I bought this thing. It was barely being held together and I ended up working all weekend to replace the two-by-fours. Ryley would sand down the wood after I finished nailing the pieces together. After she stained it, I carved our initials into the side. It's the first thing I feel for when I sit down now and it's enough of a relief to know that they're still there.

Carole sits down on one side of me while Ryley is on the other. My knee automatically moves to touch Ryley's leg. I try not to smile when she presses back, but this kind of shit makes me happy.

Cara chooses to sit next to Ryley and part of me wants to thank her, but I don't know if she's doing it because they're friends or if she's trying to keep Nate from sitting there. When Nate sits across from her, I wonder if he'll reach out to her after we're done here today. Does he have residual feelings for her? Will she be his back-up plan? It's what I want if it gives Ryley a clear conscience. I know she's afraid of hurting Nate, but her indecisiveness is slowly killing me.

McCoy sits down next to Cara and River is the last to sit down, taking the seat across from him. Cara starts talking first, recounting what she told me last night and we all start taking notes. I have everything memorized but still write things down. I'm hoping that if I read over everything multiple times it'll start making sense. Right now, it's just a bunch of names that mean nothing.

"I think I'd like to hear about the day you guys got orders," Cara says, knowing that she's asking us to break our silence. Thing is, we shouldn't, but we haven't seen our Captain since we got back. No one has called us in. We haven't been debriefed and honestly, shit is just weird. There's a Senator running around town, which could be connected or could just be completely random. The Naval Special Warfare Group 1 Commander is lurking, which I find odd only because he's refusing to question us. And if there's something up with O'Keefe, where's the investigation?

McCoy, River and I look at each other. Cara knows some things, but not much and truthfully, *we* don't even know everything. We don't ask a lot of questions when orders are given. We expect that the information we're provided is the best and not meant to harm us. We expect to encounter hostiles. We expect to exchange gunfire. We expect to be tested to the best of our abilities. We expect to come home. When you put all those together, our mission was exactly as it was meant to be, except for the amount of time it took and why.

Maybe that's the question, why were we gone for so long on something that seems so simple? Why weren't we relieved of our duty to have others take our place? I know I asked many times when we were going home. Hell, every time we met for extraction, more orders were given. After a while, you stop asking. You start trying to think ahead of your enemy and figure out their next move and beat them to it. You do anything you can to get home.

Before you know it, time is one continuous moment. One month turned into two, two into four and four into a year. O'Keefe made it possible for me to call home when Ryley had EJ, but I could never get through. I haven't asked her about that, but now I'm wondering if her number had changed. Was she being so bothered by the news that she needed to shut her life off from them? Or did the number I dialed never go anywhere? Was this mission a set-up to hide something bigger?

I look around at my family and team and know that I'm

about to sing like a canary. I want to know who ruined our lives and I want them to pay.

Before I can say anything, River speaks. "Christina Charlotte's daughter had been kidnapped," he says, keeping his voice calm. "We were told only the specifics and where to find her. O'Keefe flew with us to Cuba, filling us in, saying we didn't have time for a debriefing. He told us that due to the upcoming election, she didn't want it in the press because it could sway voters. We knew when we landed that this would be hard, but O'Keefe kept saying it would be an easy snatch and grab. We weren't to open fire, just sneak in and get her.

"When we found her, she was tied to a chair and had been beaten. McCoy went through the window and was able to get her out of there before anyone saw us, but the extraction didn't happen. Hiding in the jungle with a ten-year old isn't the easiest thing to do, especially when she doesn't know if she can trust us, she's hungry and wants her dad."

"That's what I found odd," McCoy says. "She kept asking for her dad when most girls would ask for their mom."

"Our ride back to the homeland didn't show up," I add. "We had to take cover and like River said, being with a kid who's scared isn't easy. McCoy stayed with her while Rask and I set up a perimeter around them and River tried to establish communications. When they realized the girl was gone, shit got crazy. They started yelling '¡Nos va matar!', 'he's going to kill us', and when the first gun went off she screamed, alerting them to our position. We hadn't realized that they had people in our area so our position had been compromised."

"Who were they referring to?" Cara asks as she scribbles across her paper.

"Tacito Renato," River states. He leans forward, clasping

his hands together and sighs. "He was the leader, but not the mastermind."

"Please continue," she says without looking at any of us. McCoy clears his throat and takes over from where River left off.

"We had to move deeper into the jungle, but that put a limit on River's ability to call for a new extraction point. We weren't supposed to be there, so it's not like we could walk into the nearest village and use their open airspace. It was weeks until River could get a valid signal and extraction was on the way. Except it wasn't. When the helo landed, O'Keefe told us that the girl had been kidnapped for a child sex ring and that there were American children from the database living there and we needed to get them," McCoy pauses and looks around. "I don't know about everyone here, but I know I speak for Archer, River and Rask when I say that we weren't leaving those kids behind and we didn't."

Ryley's ankle wraps around mine in a show of love or support, either way I'll take it. Having her support means everything to me. I never wanted to miss a single day with her, she knows that and missing EJ's birth was never on my list of things to do. I know that, had I not been on deployment, the Navy would've done everything to make sure I was there or at least on the phone with her.

Carole clears her throat at the same time Cara starts to speak. My eyes go from one woman to the other, waiting to see who will speak first. Carole nods, giving Cara the green light.

"I want to make sure I've heard you guys correctly. You say that you were sent to Cuba to retrieve Abigail Chesley, daughter of former Vice President Christina Charlotte?"

"What do you mean former?" River asks.

"I don't think we knew that she was even elected," I add.

This time it's Carole who speaks. "She was elected and died in a car crash about five weeks ago."

"When did you return?" Cara asks Nate.

"My team left six weeks ago, paving the way for SEAL Team 3 to return without any question," Nate replies, effectively giving us all something to think about.

chapter 23
Nate

LISTENING TO THE GUYS RECOUNT their mission, knowing that they shouldn't be doing so, I can't help but feel thankful that they are giving more credence to my statement that something is up. Once the girl was back in our custody they should've been out of there. Evan would've been home a week later and planning his and Ryley's wedding. He would've been home the day Ryley went into labor and inside the delivery room with her, holding her hand. I still would've been pacing because my nephew was being born, but she would've had him by her side where he belongs.

And now I'm questioning whether I belong with her or not.

Logic says that Evan called Cara and brought her here to come between Ryley and me, but I know that's not possible. If I didn't know how to get ahold of her, neither did he, but I can't help the fact that it was my first thought. Bringing her here falls in line with his promise of fighting dirty to win.

I never thought I'd be happy to see Cara again. It sounds bad, but the way things ended between us wasn't something I want to remember. Seeing her standing in the doorway brought back a lot of memories. I met her when she was still in college at a small coffee shop near base. She was here on spring break from Harvard, a poli-sci major hoping to get a job with the CIA. I asked her why she was here in San Diego and not Florida and she said she needed peace and calm from the long winters in Boston, not bikinis and booze.

When I met her I didn't fumble over my words, in fact I didn't really say much at all. She approached me as I sat in the corner reading the newspaper asking me if I was military and that if I was, if she could interview me for her term paper. Here she was, on vacation and doing homework. Cara sounded just like me and was everything I was looking for but didn't know it.

We saw each other every day for a week until she left. Our relationship wasn't romantic at that point, but it was a definite friendship. She was easy to talk to and she made me laugh. When I deployed, she sent packages once a month and wrote me every day, telling me about school, her day and asking if I'd be back in time for summer vacation. I wasn't going to be but that didn't stop us from talking all the time. I called her when I could because hearing her voice gave me comfort. Most of my calls went to voicemail in the beginning. She was busy. I knew that. Cara comes from money and was one of those high society girls at Harvard, attending social events all the time. Coupled with her busy caseload, a phone conversation with her was just about impossible.

It was her letters that made me fall in love with her and

two years after we met, when I had an R&R, I flew to Boston and told her how I felt. It was something that had to be done in person and not on voicemail or in a letter. I had her class schedule memorized and I waited outside the Knafel building for her to come out. I sat there with roses in my hand, dressed in my dress whites and smiling like a crazy fool in love.

Telling her was risky. I wasn't sure how she felt since we never ventured into that territory, but I knew how I felt. I thought about her every day and couldn't wait for my tour to be over so we could spend some quality time together.

When she walked out of the building, she froze. Her girlfriends giggled and told her that if she didn't say yes, that they'd be more than willing to marry me. I wasn't even thinking about marriage, I just wanted to tell her that I loved her and hoped she wanted to get coffee with me.

She did and after graduation moved to San Diego, getting a job with Navy Intelligence. It wasn't what she wanted, but we talked about her future being in Virginia and when I re-enlisted we'd ask for transfers to the east coast. Being in Intelligence allowed her to hone her craft.

Then Evan died and everything changed.

Cara knew I wouldn't leave San Diego with Ryley and my brother's unborn child here. She never asked. What she *did* ask was for me to be done. To not re-enlist... to not leave her like Evan left Ryley but I couldn't do that. I tried. I tried, but hated it. I missed being out there with my Team, my brothers. I yearned to protect my country. Ryley encouraged me to go back, against everyone's wishes, and I did so knowing that Cara would leave me. The warrior in me thought she'd stay and when she couldn't, I let her go. She moved to Washington DC, landing her dream job with the CIA and I refused to be the one to hold her back.

Now I'm sitting across from her and all I can think about is how everything in my life became so fucked up that she came back to help, except she didn't because she's just doing her job. To her, we're nothing more than an assignment.

Cara speaks with poise and confidence, showing that her education has paid off. I was always afraid I was holding her back from her true potential. That she was here to appease me because of my career. She was right to leave me. Being a SEAL's wife is no way to live when you have your own dreams and aspirations.

As the facts as we know them are laid out in front of us, I'm one hundred percent positive that the training mission my team was just on was all for show. It was to keep us, or more specifically *me*, away so that Evan could return to Ryley. Some sick bastard is playing with our lives and I want to know who it is and why.

"My team left six weeks ago, paving the way for fire team from SEAL Team 3 to return without any question," I say, adding in my own theory. "We were on a training mission in the desert, the Mojave Desert, I believe. We weren't that far from base. O'Keefe went with us, which I thought odd, but with the recent cuts by the President I didn't think too much of it until now. O'Keefe told us we were preparing for deployment, that when we came back we'd have a week or two to get our affairs in order and say goodbye.

"The first half of the month we sat in a room staring at maps of the Middle East and going over strategies. It was our last day there, but I didn't know it and we were out in the field, lying in the sand waiting for the training mission to start. We'd been out there for two days, waiting. The call came in that the exercise was over. A yellow flag went up, but no one would listen. The Team was just excited to get back home, get their business taken care of and prepare for deployment. When we got back to base, I should've trusted my instincts when I said something was up.

"Someone was giving commands, but I don't know who. They came through to Tex. He relayed the information. The first was that we were breaking down and heading back to camp. The second came in that there was no debriefing. No one questioned it but me. The other guys didn't seem to care. I have one guy going through a divorce and another who is trying to figure out if he's going to be a dad. One can say these guys were just eager to get home and get shit settled before we left – I can't say that. Sitting here, listening to everything and after doing my own research, I have no doubt that someone set SEAL Team 3 up, and I want to know why."

"That's why we're here, Nate." My name rolls off her tongue like it used to when she wanted something. I used to be able to tell by the way she said it what she wanted. Short and high-pitched, she had good news. Short and firm, I was in trouble or she was about to tell me something serious. Soft and drawn out, she wants something and something could be anything.

And right now I want to know what that anything is. Is she only interested in this case because of who it involves? Or was she assigned this case? I want to know. I should be angry with her, but I'm not. She walked out on our life together because she couldn't deal with my job. Yet, here I sit across from her and wonder how much I missed. Was staying here worth it? Looking at Evan and Ryley sitting by each other, they look at one another trying not to cause suspicion, but to an outsider they look like two people having an affair. You can see the pull they have between them. If electricity had a visual, then they would be it. I know Ryley won't do that to me, but what am I doing to her? Have I been a constant reminder of what she lost? Did I put my life on hold because I was afraid to let my brother go, hanging on to the last piece of him?

My life with Cara was fun, exciting and worth the heartache. I sought solace in Ryley because she was an easy transition. The door was always open and I was always welcomed. It was Ryley who lent me her shoulder to cry on when I needed it. I tried not to let the fact that Cara left get to me, but it hurt. I failed her when I promised that I'd always be there for her.

And now she's here for me when I didn't ask her to be. I don't care if this is her job or not. My first love has walked back into my life when it's in complete turmoil and, for the time being, I want to be done talking about this mission so I can take her aside and ask her how she's been. I want to know what she's been up to and all that she's accomplished. And in some strange, perverse way, I want to know if she's single. Has she found someone to love her the way she deserves to be loved?

The conversation continues around us and I watch Cara in action. She has papers spread out in front of us, pictures of faces that I don't know. Her words are muffled, and it's as if my head is under the water and she's standing above me talking. She tried that once when we were in Hawaii. I let her push me under and she stood above me, laughing.

When we took the trip to Hawaii, I was planning on asking her to marry me. The ring was in our hotel room and the dinner had been planned. Then the phone call came in about Evan and it was over. I put my anger and hurt before her and shouldn't have. Cara should've been the most important person in my life at that point. She was. I just didn't know how to show her.

"Nate, are you listening?"

"I'm sorry, swee... Cara. What did you say?" I catch myself before I call her sweetie, the nickname I had for her when we were together. I swallow hard as she smiles before turning away. I don't know if I should read into anything, but I think I finally know what Ryley is going through with being torn between the two of us.

chapter 24
Evan

"What was your favorite animal today?" I ask EJ, as I tuck him in. He asked me to read him a bedtime story after he had his bath and I was more than happy to take on the task. I can't imagine what he's thinking with this whole "Dad" business, especially as Nate was here last night and I'm here tonight. If I'm confused, he must be as well.

"The edapants," he says, turning over to face me. I'm over six feet tall, laying in a twin bed and EJ laughs at me because my feet hang over the edge, but I don't care. I've never felt more comfortable than I do now. He'll never know what this means to me. These moments with him are slowly starting to fill the holes in my heart. I can understand why Nate is so unwilling to let him go.

EJ shows me his bear. He holds it up, pretending it's talking to me as he tells me about the zoo. He doesn't know this, or maybe he does, but he sleeps with my teddy bear. I never understood why my mom held on to certain toys, but

I'm thankful this particular one ended up with my son. The poor bear is ratty looking, but Ryley says he doesn't go to bed without it.

"I like the elephants too," I tell him. "Did you know they bring good luck?"

"That's silly."

"I know, but it's true. I think that maybe we should buy one and put it in your backyard because we can all use some good luck."

EJ laughs and it's the most magical sound I've ever heard. "Mommy would be so mad when he poops in the backyard."

Now it's my turn to laugh right along with him. "Yeah, I think she would. Do you think she'd make me clean it up?"

He nods animatedly. "I can help if we get one."

What I wouldn't give to bring home an elephant for my son, just so I can see the look in his eyes. "I'll see what I can do."

"Goodnight, Eban."

"Goodnight, EJ."

EJ snuggles into his pillow with his arm wrapped tightly around my bear and closes his eyes. I don't want to leave, but spending time with Ryley is just as important. I don't know if I'm coming or going with her right now. My mind is telling me to run. To run fast and far without looking back because looking back holds too much pain, and I'm so tired of feeling broken. But my heart is telling me that she deserves another chance and that her mistake in telling EJ that I was his dad without me there was done out of stress and nerves. My heart is telling me to fight for her, show her that she is still my one and only even if she already knows it.

A light caress startles me awake. As my eyes focus, I see EJ is sound asleep, but feel her behind me. I know it's her by the smell of her perfume. Looking at her over my shoulder, the soft glow from EJ's night-light casts her in a shroud of gold.

"Hey," she says quietly, stepping away from the bed as I move to sit up. "I thought I'd wake you in case you wanted to go to bed."

"With you?" I ask, knowing I don't deserve or even expect an answer. I'm a smartass. I get it. I follow her out of EJ's room and down the stairs. The lights are off, but the TV is illuminating the room. It's a peaceful calm that I haven't felt in a long time. "Where's Livvie?"

"She went with Nate. She said she hadn't spent much time with him since he came back." Ryley sits down on the couch, pulling a blanket over her legs. I know I have a few options here: I can go upstairs and try to sleep, knowing I won't be able to. I can sit down next to her and try and soak up as much Ryley as possible. Or, my favorite option, I can carry her off to her room and make love to her.

While option three is what I truly want to do, I know she won't allow us to be that way and I respect that even if it's killing me. Option two is going to win out because I need her like my body needs water. I'm a fool to think I can walk away from her. I'm a stupid man if I think I can live without her in my life. I told myself in the beginning that I was going to fight dirty and I'm going to start by reminding her how much she loves me.

Rubbing my hand over my chest, I laugh when Ryley's eyes go wide. It's nice to know I still have an effect on her. Lord knows she sends me into a tailspin each time I think about her or she walks into the room. I keep my eyes on her as I move toward her. Her tongue wets her lips, telling me that everything that I've questioned about how she feels about me is wrong. She wants me, she's just torn, and I'm going to help put her back together.

I pull my shirt over my head and toss it onto the couch. Her eyes roam from my face to my body. Seeing her pull her lower lip in between her teeth is all the encouragement I need. My steps are calculated as I walk toward her. I flick the top button of my shorts, earning an inhale from her. Watching her react to me is such an ego boost. She has no idea what she does to me.

When I reach her, I pull the blanket away from her bare legs. I need to feel her skin against mine. I want the burn, the ache that she brings when she touches me. My thumb caresses her lower lip and I lean in, brushing my lips across hers. I lost track of when I got to kiss her last and right now it feels like the first time. I can taste the raspberry and chocolate ice cream that coats her mouth and feel the familiar spark when my warm tongue meets her ice cold one.

Ryley Clarke was made for me, there's no doubt about it.

Her hands hold my face to hers with her fingers adding the right amount pressure to my jaw. She's pulling me down on top of her and I'm not one to deny her what she wants. Everything moves in slow motion until her back touches the couch and she wraps her legs around me. My mind races at the thought of what I could do to her in this position if only she'd choose me. If only she'd tell me that I'm the one she wants for the rest of her life. If only she'd let me remind her of our connection and how much I love her.

My lips explore her body as I nip and taste my way over her skin. Her neck invites me to mark her, to tell everyone who sees her that she is mine, but I won't do that to her. And when her hips buck against mine I give her the pressure that she needs. I haven't dry humped this woman since she was seventeen years old, but if that's what she needs right now, who am I to say no?

Sharp nails dig into my back as I move against her. My freaking balls are going to be purple at this rate, but I don't care. Ryley angles herself so that I have no choice but to kiss her. I'm not complaining. I'll happily kiss her until the sun comes up and sets again if that's what she needs from me.

I push against her and swallow her moans as she rocks against me. I love how her body responds to me... the eagerness of needing to be connected, showing me that it belongs to me as it molds against me. It's been far too many years since we've even come close to being like this, but I haven't forgotten her signs. I clutch her hands in mine; my anchor to keep from touching her because I know if I do there will be no stopping me. I pull away from her so I can look in her eyes when she lets go. It's a face I only have in my memories and after so many years apart, that memory has faded.

Green eyes stare a back at me, eyes that first caught my attention years ago. She knows what I'm waiting for and is willing to submit to me as I continue to rock against her. Her back arches off the couch and her eyes close briefly.

"Do you need this from me?" I ask her, whispering into her ear. She nods as I move faster until I feel her legs squeeze my hips and her body tenses. Ryley seeks my mouth to bury her cries as our clothed bodies slide against each other. After the tension in her legs subsides, I kiss down her neck and over her shoulder, across the top of her breasts until her breathing evens out.

Disengaging from her is the last thing I want, but falling

asleep on top of her might not be met with a round of applause in the morning either. Adjusting myself, I roll onto my side, bringing her with me. Trailing my fingers over her cheekbone, I seek reassurance in her eyes. It's there, but I still need the words. I still need her to tell me that I'm the one she wants.

"That was unexpected," I tell her hoping that she doesn't come back with something off the wall like, "well Nate and I did that last night so I'm just testing out my options" because if she did, I'd die right here and now.

"I'm sorry. I know you must be frustrated with me."

Oh, she has no idea. "I'm not, Ry. I know you need time." I say as I wrap her in my arms.

She pushes back slightly, with her hand on my chest. "I need you to know something, Evan. The day in the park, it wasn't what you thought. EJ asked if you were his dad and I couldn't lie to him. Not anymore. I've been lying to him for five years and when he looked me in the eye and asked if Eban was his dad I just lost it. I'm so sorry that you weren't there."

"Me too," I say, pulling her to my chest. This is how we fall asleep, with me holding her and her leg in between mine. This is how we used to sleep when I'd visit her at school or she'd come to the base on the weekends. We'd fall asleep like this the night before I'd deploy or leave on missions.

The last time I held her like this, I didn't see her for six years.

I hated leaving Ryley and EJ this morning, but in my

haste to make sure she wasn't alone with Nate any longer than necessary yesterday, I forgot to bring any clothes over with me. River and Frannie are gone when I arrive, and I honestly feel uncomfortable being here when they're not home. Although, had I known the house would be empty, I'd probably have had Cara meet me here and let her snoop around. I'm still not convinced that Frannie was just pining away, thinking her husband would return any moment. I can understand her keeping things around the house – hell, Ryley did it, too – but there definitely wasn't fresh beer in the fridge when I showed up.

Then there's the note threatening Ryley's life that showed up at the house. Only Frannie, Lois and Carter knew we'd be there and the note was clearly meant for us. Adding the word "she" was the mistake made there. A message meant to scare us into stopping our own investigation is done the opposite way so it has only spurred us on. If those three are our suspects, I'd easily eliminate Lois and Carter unless they're in some type of trouble, but I doubt that. I don't see Carter doing anything to hurt Ryley. Frannie is the wildcard in my mind, but I can't pinpoint why and that bothers me.

Turning on the water, I undress as it warms up. Stepping in, the hot water burns my skin, but the pain is welcomed. It reminds me that I'm alive and for that I'm thankful. Call it a hazard of the job, but there's been too many times in my life that I have had thoughts about death. Just this once I want to feel like no one is behind me, lurking in the shadows. I know it's a lot to ask, considering what I've been through.

I wash quickly, wanting to get back to Ryley. It's not that I need to be there to protect her, that's a given. I need to be with her, feel her presence. Having her near is like fuel for my soul.

She's the sunshine in my life, even when it's raining.

After drying off, I use my towel to clean the fogged over bathroom mirror. I'm in need of a shave and a decent haircut. While we were gone we each took turns shaving each other's heads with our knives. Not the smartest thing to do, but effective nonetheless. I think I'll call Jensen and see if EJ and I can meet him today so we can head down to the barbershop and get us all a clean shave. EJ, of course, will just get to play in the shaving cream.

Once I'm dressed, I'm back in the bathroom cleaning up after myself. This is another reason why I don't like staying here. I feel like I'm intruding and don't want to leave a mess. If I were at Ryley's I wouldn't worry about wiping everything down and making sure the sink is clean after I've brushed my teeth. I open the door to the cabinet under the sink to find any type of cleaning product possible. I feel like a creeper, invading their privacy.

Spotting the cleaner, I reach for it, knocking over a stack of towels. My heart stops when I see a black cell phone with a red blinking light. I pick it up and hold it in my hand, turning it over and wishing that my eyes were deceiving me. What would a cell phone — and not just any cell phone, but a Blackberry — be doing hiding in between a stack of towels in the bathroom?

The phone vibrates and the screen illuminates, alerting whoever this belongs to that they have a new message. My finger hovers over the OK button, knowing that if I look I'll be breaking the trust of River and Frannie. However, I know if I don't look I'll always suspect that Frannie is somehow involved in our mess.

Sitting against the tub, I press the button and the message pops up.

They're getting close. Feds are in town.

I've always been the type of warrior to see things for what they are and I'm seeing this for exactly what it is. Someone in this house knows more than they're saying and as much as I want to sit here and read through these messages, I need to get this to someone I trust. Locking the screen I slide the phone into my pocket and fix the towels. Someone is going to come looking for this phone and know it's gone, but I'm okay with that because I'll be ready for their next move.

The last thing I do before leaving River's is grab my stuff. If I have to stay in a hotel, then so be it, but I can't stay in this house knowing that either one of them could be involved. My money is on Frannie, but why? Why would she do something like this and for what?

That's what I have to find out.

My options are limited. I can't go to base and give this to Carole; I don't trust anyone there. Nate is likely on base as he's still on active duty so that leaves Cara, except I don't have a phone to call her with and that means going back to Ryley's. I really need to get a cell phone because trying to be James Bond without one is cramping my style.

As soon as I pull into Ryley's driveway, Nate pulls in behind me. Normally, I'd be seeing red, but right now he can help. I get out of the car and walk toward him. He gets out, with his hands up.

"I know it's your day, but after listening to everyone last night you have to know that I want to help."

"I know," I say, shocking even myself.

"You do?"

"Yes, and I have a ticking time bomb in my pocket, but I'm not sure this is a safe place to talk. I saw a few nondescript black cars before I pulled in and call me suspicious all you want because I am."

"What's the bomb?" he asks.

"Random device with a few messages that need to be read," I say, looking around.

Nate nods and pulls out his phone. "Let me call Jensen and have him come over to stay with Ryley."

That's probably the first thing I've heard him say since I've been back that I agree with. While he's on the phone, I run into the house. Ryley and EJ are in the kitchen. He's coloring and she's dancing around, moving her body to the music playing through the radio. As much as I'd love to stay and watch, I can't. Grabbing her by the waist, she lets out a little yelp until her eyes meet mine.

"Do me a favor?"

"Anything," she says, out of breath.

"Lock every god damn door and window in this house and set your alarm. Make sure Deefur is with you at all times and go get your gun and keep it near you. Your dad is on his way over. Do *not* open the door for anyone but him, Nate or me. Am I clear?" I say into her ear, thankful that the radio can drown me out. "I'll be with Nate," I say. I pull away in time to see a small smile play on her lips. I know this is what she wants, but she really shouldn't read into anything.

Holding her chin between my thumb and forefinger I look for any sign that she's afraid. It's there, but she knows how to be a warrior. She's strong.

"I love you." I kiss her quickly before stopping in front of EJ.

Leaning in, I say, "Remember when you went and hid from Nate the other day?" he nods so I continue. "If your mom tells you to do that, you go and don't come out until me, Nate or Grandpa comes to get you, okay?" He nods and runs to Ryley.

I hate that they're scared, but they need to be on alert. I blow them both kisses and motion to the windows, reminding her to lock them. If Frannie is involved, she's had unlimited access to this house and for all I know it's bugged.

Nate's in his car when I come out and I hurry over, sliding into the passenger seat. "Jensen is on his way and Carole and Cara are meeting us."

"Where are we going?" I ask, as he pulls out of the driveway. My eyes are on every car we pass as we drive down the road.

"To the one place they least expect you to show up."

chapter 25
Nate

THIS IS HOW EVAN'S HOMECOMING should've been – him and I running off to hang out, doing the brotherly thing - but that's not the case. The only reason he's in my car right now is because we have the same agenda… to find out who is behind everything. "Everything" is such a broad word when you think about it, but how else do you describe it? From what I can tell there are multiple players involved and each one is hiding something different from us.

When I pull into the cemetery, I expect Evan to balk but he doesn't. He just looks out of the window without saying a word. I stop in front of his grave and get out, leaving him to follow. With my hands pushed into my pockets, I glare at his tombstone for the lies that it holds.

"I'm never going to expect that you'll understand about Ryley and me. Sometimes I don't even understand it. But when you died, a piece of me died with you. All I had left was your unborn child. Twins have a special bond and as of late I have questioned that bond, but I know now that I used EJ to fill the void... *the emptiness*... that your death left me with.

"The day we buried you, it poured. Mom didn't want to have a burial outside, but I wouldn't let you go into that ground without a proper goodbye. I flinched each time the rifles went off and bloodied my hand when I pounded my Trident into your coffin. I stayed until you were lowered in. I was here when the sexton covered you with dirt. For one week I laid vigil next to you because you didn't have a tombstone and I needed everyone who walked by to know that you were my brother, that you lost your life fighting for this country and that I had lost my best friend.

"You asked me when were eighteen to protect that girl, knowing full well how I felt about her. I loved her, Evan, and I still do, but it's not the same love the two of you share. I was there, though. I picked her up off the ground. I made her eat so the baby could grow. So that she could have a piece of you forever, so that I had someone in my life that represented my brother. I was selfish in every way possible, and yet I don't regret it.

"She's just so damn easy to love, Evan. It was hard not to fall for her after Cara left. Everything that I was to her, she was to me in return when Cara walked out of my life. She rebuilt me when I was a broken man and she did so by loving and treating me as her equal.

"I know what you're going through when you look at EJ. This little baby that I held hours after he was born was my one link to you. I vowed to protect him with everything that I am and will continue to do so until the day I die. The day he called me 'Daddy', I cried. I was on my knees, crying right here asking for your help, asking for you to tell me what to do, to give me a sign that everything was going to be okay.

"But nothing was okay. Cara was gone. She left me because I re-enlisted. She didn't want to lose me the same way Ryley lost you, so walking away was easier for her. I asked Ryley what to do and she didn't know. Her heart never healed after losing you. We were two lost people trying to raise a little boy who saw his little daycare friends call the other men in their lives 'Dad'. He just followed them.

"Ryley and I haven't been together that long. I'm assuming she told you that, but if she hasn't, you can hear it from me. It was years, Evan, before she'd look at me, let alone another man. There would be days that she wouldn't move from the couch, usually around your birthday, anniversary or the date you died. Songs would bring her to her knees or EJ would do something that reminded her of you and she'd be right back in a funk.

"I'm not her magic cure, I didn't make missing you any easier. I'm just the guy who knew how she felt and was willing to love her regardless of her loving another man. I know I'll never be number one in her heart and that's something I knew when things started changing for us. But seeing her smile, hearing her laughter after a corny joke, or watching her eyes light up when she had good news was worth every bit of herself that she shared with me."

Birds chirp around us, keeping the awkward silence at bay. Evan sighs heavily next to me as we stand over his grave. The flowers that I brought when I returned have wilted and are falling over. His American flag is off center, likely from the landscapers. I want to fix it, but at the same time I don't know if the man buried in the coffin is worthy of a flag. I don't even know if there's a body in there.

"Are you going to let her go?" It's not the question I thought he'd ask, and frankly I don't have an answer for him. I sigh and keep my gaze on the ground.

"I still hate you," he says after a moment, "but I understand. Thank you for telling me."

I nod due to the lack of words I have to say right now.

"Is that why you brought me here?"

"No, I've needed to say that to you for a while, but we're never alone and the last time we were was after you tried to kill me in a bar fight." I laugh, but the situation we're in isn't funny. "I brought you here because if we're being followed or trailed, they're not going to look for you here. The last place, at least in my opinion that a man wants to go hang out at is his grave. Cara and Carole are on their way here."

"Tell me about Cara?" he asks as a slight smile forms on my face. Just like Ryley is Evan's favorite subject, at one point Cara was mine. Some habits, like smiling when I hear her name, are hard to break.

I shake my head. "You died and everything changed. Being a SEAL's wife didn't appeal to her anymore so she left and I let her go. I didn't ask her to stay because the rejection, I think, would've been worse and I didn't want to hold her back either."

"The letters that I received, they never talked about Cara. I was so happy to hear from Ryley that I didn't think about what Cara was doing or what you were doing. Hell, I didn't even know that Carter and Lois had a kid until the other day. I wrote you, though. And O'Keefe assured me that you knew what was going on... that you were keeping Ryley safe."

Looking at Evan as he stares at his grave makes me wish

he had those letters. "He lied. I know you don't want to believe me, but I'm telling you the truth. If I knew what was going on, I would've done something. Carole would've done something. After you died, she looked into everything, trying to figure out why you guys were over there and found nothing." I shift my stance, kicking some grass as I do. "Do you remember any of those letters?"

He looks up and shakes his head. "I wish. I memorized the important things like EJ's birthday. Sometimes the letters were short, others were long. They were all typed. Then there would be months when we wouldn't get anything and now that I think about, we'd ask about getting the hell out of there and suddenly a box would come. We'd get pictures, letters, sometimes clothes and our favorite foods all days later after asking. It was like whoever was behind this had a team with them. I don't know."

The crunching of gravel sounds around us, causing us both to look. Cara and Carole get out of their shared car and make their way over to us. Carole stands next to Evan, while Cara takes my side and even though it's been years since she and I have been together, the urge to grab her hand is there. I'm thankful I've left my hands in my pockets or I'd have some explaining to do.

"Why are we here?"

"Thought we'd dig up my body," Evan says as he laughs, earning a slap from Carole and an eye roll from Cara. "Sorry, I found this under some towels in the bathroom at River's house. As I was holding it a text message came in. I haven't looked at the messages on there because honestly it's been some time since I've touched a cell phone and I didn't want to risk erasing something." He holds the Blackberry in the palm of his hand and the indicator light blinks rapidly.

"There are more messages or alerts," Cara says as I look at her questioningly. "What? Mine blinks like that." She says, shrugging.

We stand around Evan and his outstretched hand as if he's holding a timer to a bomb. I don't know if we're waiting for it to go off again or what, but none of us are moving.

"Evan," Carole says his name so calmly, I feel like she's about to deliver bad news. "Have you prepared yourself for the possibility that we could look at that and find out that River is involved?"

He shakes his head, clasping his fingers over the phone. "I don't think he's involved."

"Why?" I ask.

"If he were, he wouldn't let me stay at his house."

"Good point," I say, looking at everyone. "I figured this is the safest place right now. I want answers. I want to know who did this to us." When I say "us", my eyes find Cara's. Last night I thought about how things would've been different. In all likelihood she and I would be married by now and living in Virginia. But someone decided to screw with my family and now they must pay.

"We could put a tap on the phone and put it back," Cara offers.

Evan shakes his head. "I want to know now."

It's been days since Carole took the cell phone from us.

We were tempted to read it all right there, but she wanted everything from it, including emails and internet searches. Carole has a friend in NCIS who is helping her, someone she trusts. The hard part was letting go of what we considered a huge piece of evidence and probably the key to discovering who is behind all of this.

I reported for work, keeping up the guise that everything is fine. A few team members had a lot of questions, but others just sat there, likely contemplating how something so fucked up happened to someone they know. Believe me, I've been asking myself the same question over and over again.

Evan didn't return to River's and I told him that he could stay with Ryley and EJ, and I'll stay at Carter's. It's not ideal, but my brother doesn't have any place to live so it is what it is… for right now. Evan also hasn't informed River, McCoy or Rask about the phone. He's not sure who he can trust right now and feels that keeping a low profile is better. The one thing he *has* done in the past few days is finally got his own cell phone.

"Is it weird?" Tex asks, interrupting my daydream. When I said I'm back to work, I am, but only in the sense that I show up on base and watch everyone, even Carole. Commander Clarke, as I refer to her when we're on base, suggested I keep my eyes and ears open and my mouth and my fingers off the keyboard. I'm doing as she says.

"Is what weird?" I ask, bending over to pick up some rope.

"Having your brother back?"

I shrug, keeping up the pretense that we're on the outs. We're not, but we're not exactly friends. He does respond to my text messages and I consider that a huge step from where we were earlier.

"I'm happy he's home, but he's trying to steal my woman." I make it sound worse than it is. Truth is, Ryley belongs to Evan and it's something that I'm slowly starting to realize. Now if only my heart would listen.

"It's not mine," he blurts out, catching me off guard.

"What isn't?" I ask as I wait for him to pick up the other section of rope. I found us grunt work to do that would put us near the building of Admiral Ingram. Tex doesn't need to know, but having an unsuspecting partner in crime is always nice.

"The baby, it's not mine."

"How do you feel about that?"

He stops mid stride, causing me to turn around. "You said being a dad is one of the greatest joys in your life, do you still feel that way knowing your brother is going to take your son away?"

I set my section down and look at Tex. "It's not that Evan will take EJ away, I'll still be there. EJ needs to know that Evan is his dad, but we're not forcing the situation. But yeah, being a dad is pretty much the best feeling in the world, why?"

Tex shrugs. "After we got back I went and saw her, and thought, 'yeah I can do this'. But then another guy comes around and he says the baby is his. So I ask her and she says it's his, but his job isn't stable and she wants us to get married so she can have benefits and all that shit."

My mouth drops open, but honestly I'm not surprised. This is one of the reasons Ryley refused to hang out with any of the girlfriends because they're intentions aren't always for the best. Hearing him say it out loud, though, really turns my stomach.

"Come on, let's get this rope stowed. I'm meeting Ryley

for lunch."

"Ah, a little lunch time nookie in the back of your car," he jokes.

"Yeah, something like that," I reply. Except it isn't and I don't expect it to be. I don't ask what goes on at the house either. I'm just hoping she's respecting the ring that she wears. As soon as we're finished, I take off in search of Ryley. We're meeting at the café near base since she refuses to even step foot past the gate.

The café is just a short jog and I find her sitting outside, waiting for me. As soon as she sees me, she stands and has a bottle of water waiting for me in her outstretched hand. I guzzle down the ice-cold water first before leaning in to give her a kiss. Our lips linger against each other's momentarily until I pull away.

"I thought we could get some ice cream and go sit on the beach."

"For lunch?"

She shrugs. "I thought it'd be something different. Besides, I already ate."

"You did?" I ask, pulling her into the café. "Why are we having lunch then?"

I tell the waitress our order and pay. For as long as I've known Ryley, she's ordered the same kind of ice cream and if the place doesn't have it, she usually goes without.

Walking side by side, both of us carrying cups of ice cream, we sit down on one of the log formations. There's a charred out fire pit which was probably done by one of my Team members or some other sailors hanging out down here.

"I had lunch with Cara today," she says in between bites. "She asked about you. In fact, she spent the entire lunch talking about you."

"Is that so?"

Ryley nods as she puts a spoonful of her favorite raspberry and chocolate ice cream in her mouth. "Mhm," she mumbles.

I finish off my cup and set it down in the sand. The ocean waves are calm, but won't be later when BUD/S training starts. I'd like to watch this new class, but I have other pressing issues to deal with.

"Ry, there's nothing going on with Cara. I've spent some time with her, but she's just trying to help us figure out what happened."

"I know," she says as she puts her cup down and pulls my hand into hers. "She loves you and I know you love her. I also know that you love me, but it's not the same. She's your Evan and we both know the only reason you're not together is because Evan died. But he's not dead anymore..."

"Ryley, are you trying to tell me that you chose Evan?"

She shakes her head. "No, Nate, I'm telling you to choose Cara." Ryley slips the ring I bought for her off her finger and places it in my hand. "I don't know what's going to happen with Evan, but I'm not going to be the one who holds you back from happiness. This decision is made wholeheartedly, Nate. There's nothing rash about it and I'm not hurt. It feels right. I love Cara, and she's the one you need in your life, not me."

Tears prick my eyes as I clutch her ring. I pull her into my arms and hold her. I don't want to admit it, but she's right. When we kissed earlier, the spark I used to feel wasn't there. It felt like I was kissing my sister. Maybe that's why I can walk away knowing everything will be okay.

When she pulls away, she kisses me, and I still only feel

her lips and nothing else. "Cara's here. She's waiting for you in the parking lot. I came with her, but my mom is here to pick me up."

I turn to look and there she is, dressed like she's going to work. I take Ryley's hand in mine and we walk back toward the street. She releases my hand and waves at Cara, but I don't take my eyes off of her until she's in Carole's car.

Putting my hands into my pockets, I walk over to Cara who greets me with a smile. We both wave when Carole honks her horn, our eyes following her car out of the parking lot. Cara steps to me and it's as if everything moves in slow motion. My head turns toward the deafening sound of metal crunching against metal, the nauseating smell of rubber on fire and the heart-shattering wail of blood curdling screams.

Carole's car is upside down in the middle of the road with flames coming out of the engine. "Call 911," I yell at Cara as I take off running toward the car. The explosion knocks me back and all I can do is scream.

chapter 26
Evan

I'LL NEVER KNOW WHAT RYLEY went through when she was told that I had died, but if it's anything like what I'm currently going through, I'm going to have to find a new way to worship this woman. Telling her I love her, or how much I want to be with her, is never going to be enough. I have never been the type of person that can describe my emotions very well and Ryley knows that but right now, pacing outside the emergency room doors that separate me from her, I'm about to use every word possible to describe how I feel. Scared, nervous, hopeful, I don't know. My body is zinging with anticipation to see her, to hear from the doctors, anything to calm my nerves. I feel like if I sit down my body will shatter into a million pieces.

When my phone rang and I saw that it was Nate, I almost didn't answer it. After having gone six years without a cell phone, I've grown used to the nice feeling of not being attached to anything. I know it's a necessity, but it's probably one that I could've lived without for a little while longer.

Nate may have come clean, twice, but it doesn't erase the fact that when I came home he had claim on my girl. I know others are to blame and if I ever find out who has done this to my family and me, the punishment will be severe.

But I answered the call and to hear Nate's broken voice on the other end was enough to stop me in my tracks. It was the first time since I've been back that I cared about what he had to say. After hearing the words, "there was an accident, but she's okay," I froze. I dropped to my knees and felt my axis shift. I just got her back. I can't lose her now.

Ryley and Carole were in a car accident. Cara and Nate were there, in the parking lot, when it happened. How or why they were all together, I don't know. I haven't asked and right now I don't care. What I *do* care about is finding the asshole responsible for running them into the semi-truck. According to Nate, Ryley and Carole drove off and not seconds later he heard the crash. He went to them, only to be knocked on his ass when the car exploded.

That wasn't enough to keep Nate down and he burnt his hand trying to save Ryley and her mom. His efforts were futile because the motherfucker who insists on trying to harm my family committed this act in front of a military base and so many sailors saw what had happened and were there before Nate. *They* saved my family. They also saved Nate before Carole's car exploded for a second time. The triage nurse that treated his hand told him that he wouldn't be here if it weren't for them.

I may be pissed at my brother. I may have hatred toward him, but I'm not ready to lose him.

I've been asked multiple times to move, but I refuse. I want to see the doctor first when he comes through the double doors. Jensen is standing next to me, helping me put up a solid "don't fuck with us" wall. Our women are back there and we need to know what's going on.

I never wanted to think that a job I love and trust would be behind whatever fuckery is going on, but the more evidence that we uncover the deeper the bullshit becomes. I have no doubt that today's accident is a result of that phone I found in River's house. He's here, waiting with the rest of my family, but Frannie isn't. I haven't asked him where she's at because I don't care. In fact, when I see her, I may strangle her until she tells me what I want to know. Hell, for all I know River could be in on this, but my gut is telling me otherwise. No one spends six years in a damn jungle by choice. As our fire team leader, he did everything possible to keep us safe and to get us home. But someone didn't want us home and we have to find out why.

If Frannie is involved, I feel sorry for River. I don't know what's worse: Finding out your girl moved on with your brother, or finding out your wife knew you were alive the whole time and played along with it. Both are pretty shitty, but his situation would be just plain fucked up.

"What's taking so long?" I groan, tapping my fist against the wall. I've never really been in a hospital until today, but I can see why people hate them. Everything is white and plastic. The chairs are uncomfortable, hard and uninviting. It's the same way I feel when I go to the therapist's office, but I'd take Doc Hudson over this place any day. When I look around, I see death. It's something I've experienced and standing here now, you see how it's affecting people. The nurses don't smile when you look at them even though they're supposed to be here to reassure loved ones. The doctors walk with their heads down to avoid eye contact with people because they can't mask the pain and agony they feel when they've lost a patient. The white walls and floral prints can't brighten a place like this.

"Precautionary measures, I'm sure," Jensen says as calmly as possible. How he can keep a cool head right now is beyond me. His wife and daughter are back there and we know nothing. We're being kept in the dark. All someone needs to do is tell us if they're okay.

Nate was in the ambulance with Ryley while Cara rode with Carole. Both of them were unconscious, battered and bleeding from the wounds on their heads, but they were alive according to Nate and Cara. I fought to go back there, to watch the doctors as they did what they had to do, just to make sure they're on my team and not working for whoever tried to kill them.

"They need to come out soon or I'm going back there." I rub my hand over the top of my head, moving my hat back and forth. My other hand holds a bear, some stupid bear that I bought for her today which I thought she'd like. Why I'm holding it now, I don't know, but something told me to bring it in when I got to the hospital.

"They've only been back there for forty minutes."

"How do you know?" I ask, looking at the man who should be my father-in-law.

"I'm timing them. I'm giving them twenty minutes to give us an update before I let my son-in-law loose."

I try not to laugh, but it's funny. He's my voice of reason right now because he knows that these double doors aren't enough to keep me away.

"Any word?" Nate asks, as he joins us. His left hand is

bandaged in white gauze.

"Nothing yet. Are you okay?" I ask, signaling down to his hand. He holds it up and nods.

"Just a burn, nothing I can't handle. I'm just sorry I didn't get there fast enough."

"You did fine. You were there for her when she needed you." I don't know why I'm giving him the affirmation he's looking for, but he did what he could. He has to know this wasn't his fault and he couldn't have prevented it. Some sick bastard is on the loose right now.

"There are people in the waiting room. Everyone is here except for Mom, she's staying with EJ," I say, but hold back on telling him that I think Frannie is involved. I don't have the proof, but everything in my mind is telling me she's guilty.

"Let me know as soon as you hear anything."

I nod and Jensen assures Nate that we'll fill him in. I won't, though, because as soon as the doctor comes out I'm going in.

"I can't lose her," I say to anyone who is within earshot to hear me.

"It was a car accident, Evan. They're both fine."

I shake my head and hold up the bear so I can look at him. He's cheesy, but Ryley will love him. "It's not that, Jensen. I can't lose her, period. This isn't some high school infatuation that I never grew out of, or the fact that she should've been waiting for me when I came home. She's who I see when I dream at night and who I want to see when I wake-up. When I think about what makes me tick, it's Ryley. She's the reason I am who I am today because without her I'm less than half a man."

Jensen sighs. "I get it, Evan, because that's how I feel about Carole."

"If she chooses me, I'm going to marry your daughter the first chance I get."

"About time," he mumbles, causing me to laugh. If he only knew that I would've married her the second I came back from my so-called "snatch and grab mission".

I quickly stop laughing when the doctor walks out. He looks somber as he takes off his paper cap. He holds it in his hand and the expression on his face is grim. Jensen steps forward first, followed by me.

"Your wife and daughter are fine. Your wife suffered a compound fracture to her femur and a broken arm. She's needs to have pins put in both her leg and arm. The ortho surgeon is with her now and will be taking her up to surgery in a few minutes. She'll be confined to a wheelchair and physical therapy will be required, but other than that she'll make a full recovery. Your daughter has fared much better than your wife. Aside from breaking her wrist, she's fine. They're very lucky that they were saved before the car was fully engulfed in flames. They have no burns, whatsoever."

I let out a huge sigh of relief that both of them are okay. I don't know how our family would cope with losing either of them. Broken bones we can deal with, those are easy. Death is not.

"How did my wife break her arm?" Jensen asks. I know he's concerned, but I want to shake him and tell him he can ask questions later. I just want to get in there. I'm trying to be patient, but my patience expired a long time ago.

"We think she put her arm across your daughter to save her." I let the words sink in. Carole saved her daughter. The thoughts filtering through my mind right now are not good. I have visions of Ryley hitting the windshield and flying through it. It's like I'm there, at the accident, even though I wasn't. I can't help but picture what could've been if they had been anywhere else and not in front of the base.

"Can I go in now?" I ask, but the doctor ignores me. Jensen looks at him, but he shakes his head.

"Only family is allowed until she's moved."

"Fuck that, I *am* her family," I say as I move past him and through the double doors. He says something about security but I don't give a shit. I *need* to see Ryley. I need to touch her, feel her skin against mine and hear her voice. I have to see for myself that every part of her is okay.

I look in every room, seeing things that I can't erase from my mind. In one room, a wife is sobbing over who I'm assuming is her husband. It didn't look so good for him. In another, there is a child with only a nurse in there. We make eye contact, and she looks sad and despondent. Where are her parents? Short of yelling out her name and drawing attention to myself, this is all I can do. Each room is either occupied or empty; sadly there are more occupants than I expected.

Finally I find her with a bandage on her forehead and her red hair tucked behind her ears. She looks pale and for her that's not a good thing. Her casted arm rests on her stomach and her eyes are closed. I try to be quiet as I walk in, but to no avail. When her eyes spring open, a small, sad smile appears on her flawless face. It changes though when she sees the bear I'm carrying.

I hold him up in front of my face and move him from side to side like he's dancing as I walk toward her. "You float my boat, Ryley Clarke." She laughs, and it's instantly like everything is okay. I know she hasn't chosen me, but that doesn't stop me from stealing a kiss from her. And as happy as I am to give her this bear, he's cramping my style because he's wedged in between us.

"I don't know, babe, I saw this guy and thought he looked like me with his sailor hat and his life buoy, but right now he's just in the way."

"I love him," she says as she pulls him into her chest with her good arm. "It's worse than it looks, Archer, I promise you." She knows that calling me Archer will soothe just about anything because for some reason hearing her call me by my last name is freaking hot.

"You scared me."

She nods as tears prick her eyes. "I was scared, but someone pulled me out of the car before... I just don't know what's going on and why people want to hurt us."

I try to hug her, but considering the bed and her arm, it's really a half-assed attempt. Her hand clutches the back of my shirt as she sobs. I want to tell her that it's going to be okay, but I don't believe those words myself and I'm not going to lie to her.

"We're uncovering the truth and someone wants that truth to stay hidden."

"Did you kill someone over there, someone powerful?" she asks as she pulls away.

"I did, but I don't know how he's connected to what's going on here. None of it makes sense, but I swear to you, Ry, I am going to find out."

chapter 27
Nate

I LIKE TO PRIDE MYSELF on being a man's man. The type that isn't afraid to open doors for women, pull out their chairs or help someone across the street. Being that type of man, I've always been the one to drive, but Cara won't let me and I'm having a hard time sitting still. It's not that she's a bad driver, I'm just used to being in control.

And right now, I'm not in control of anything.

It's been almost two weeks since Carole turned the mysterious cell phone over and the car accident happened. I never wanted to hand the phone over to NCIS but Cara and Carole thought it would be best, especially since it was found in the home of a serviceman. I thought with Cara being here she could look into it, but she reminded me that she's investigating Lawson and it would be best to follow Carole's lead.

The witnesses from the car accident couldn't provide many details. A black SUV-type vehicle was the only consistent evidence. Some saw a license plate, others said there wasn't one. A few said the sun was shining too brightly and they couldn't see anything other than the SUV speeding away. This is a police matter and because Ryley and Carole escaped, the police are slow moving. If I were them I'd be overturning every auto body shop possible from here to Mexico.

Since that day at the beach, Ryley has reminded me each and every day to tell Cara how I feel. At first, I wanted to tell Ryley that she was wrong, that she's the one I love, but words failed me. I *do* love Ryley, but we would've never been together had this shit with Evan not happened. I'd like to think that Cara and I would be married by now. She was happy in our life before and it makes me wonder if I can make her happy again.

I'm not hiding the fact that I'm staring at her while she drives us to the NCIS office and by the devilish little smile that she has on her face, I can tell she knows it. Does she know what I'm thinking? Do I even know what I'm thinking? As I look at her, I see the same beautiful, smart, sexy and vivacious woman that I fell in love with years ago. Her brown hair is shorter, but with the same blonde highlights that she used to fret over when we were together. Her make-up is still subtle and you only know she's wearing it if you look hard enough. Her lips are still painted in the soft muted pink that she used all the time. She'd always buy multiple tubes for fear she would run out and the store wouldn't have it. I used to call her "cotton candy" because her lips were always pink and they tasted so sweet.

The only notable difference in her now, aside from the poise in which she carries herself, is the gun on her hip. And call me stupid, but I find that incredibly sexy. There's something enticing about taking a woman to a gun range and firing off a few rounds.

I'm not sure if what I'm feeling now is anticipation or anxiousness, but sitting here thinking about her isn't helping. I should be thinking about Ryley. Weeks ago she was my fiancée and now she's not. I know for a fact she's single and hasn't told Evan because she wasn't sure if jumping back in with two feet was the smartest thing to do. Over breakfast this morning, she told me she feels like her heart has been ripped out of her chest one too many times and while she loves Evan, she wonders if it's enough to make them work. Six years of thinking the one you love is dead when he really wasn't is a hard pill to swallow. I told her she has to do what's right for her and that Evan would understand. I know he would, but he may not like it.

Ryley's words are on automatic replay, "I'm telling you to choose Cara." To me, Ryley is a selfless woman, giving up what could be her happiness for another woman that she calls a friend. I should heed the words from Ryley, but I'm not sure Cara is in the same mind frame and even if she were, the logistics of our lives would be the forefront of our relationship. I have to ask myself if Cara is worth giving it all up. Is the love I feel… *felt*… is it worth leaving Coronado and starting over in Virginia?

The car comes to a halt and I glance quickly to see that we're stopped on the highway. Traffic is the bane of existence in the State of California.

"Your staring is starting to creep me out." She looks over at me, raising her eyebrow.

"Do you remember what it feels like?"

"What *what* feels like?"

"What it feels like when I kiss you?" I ask, not giving her time to respond as I reach over and cup her face with my hands. We crash into each other with hungry, eager lips. It's sloppy and hard as our tongues battle for dominance, intertwining in an intense dance. Fingernails dig into my skin as she clutches the front of my shirt, pulling me toward her. Our seatbelts strain as we fight to get closer. I always thought that Ryley and I had chemistry, but I was wrong. In this moment, I'm certain I am meant to be with Cara.

Our kisses turn soft, less eager, but with more passion. Her hands move from my chest and onto my neck as her fingertips play with my earlobes. Horns honk in the background causing her to pull away, but not before I get another taste of her lips. I don't know about her, but I'm having a hard time catching my breath and when she pulls away, the pink flush of her cheeks tells me she felt something too.

Cara smiles as she faces forward and starts moving with the flow of traffic. It dawns on me that her car wasn't in park and we just made out in the middle of a traffic jam on the highway. I'm back to staring at her because I can't get enough of her. After one kiss, I already want more.

Maybe I never stopped wanting more.

"Stop staring," she says with a hint of laughter in her voice.

"I can't help it," I tell her honestly. "You're still the most beautiful girl in the world to me. I don't think that will ever change."

She looks at me briefly before turning back to the road.

"Do you have any regrets?" she asks causing me to turn away. I'm a man with many regrets, but they don't define me. I know I have to tell her the truth.

"I regret letting you leave, Cara," I respond without hesitation. After that, words fail me. I want to ask her to stay here, to test us out and see if we have a future, but that would be unfair to her.

Cara looks off into the distance, avoiding eye contact. Her hands fidget, moving over the steering wheel. "You and Ryley —" I stop her before she can continue. I need to take a page out of Evan's book and play dirty here.

"Cara, what Ryley and I had was different from what I shared with you. Ryley was there when everything happened and EJ was my link to Evan. I planned to marry her because I felt it gave her and EJ what they were missing. I love her, but not like I love you. Seeing you the other day, every letter we wrote, every kiss we shared, it was like it was yesterday. I want that again, if you do. I want the chance to show you that we're not a mistake that we're meant to be together. I want to continue what we started and create the kind of life we talked about having."

"I want that too," she says as she looks at me quickly. With those four words I know I'm on the path to my future.

Cara sits while I pace. Never in my life did I expect to find myself in the NCIS office. As a sailor, it's a place that you never want to visit. If you're here it's because you either saw something, or did something. I've worked my ass off to always do right by the code in which I live. Except I feel like I've failed my brother. I should've known that he was alive, but I masked those feelings with EJ. I used my son... *nephew*... to fill in the gap that wasn't missing, but broken. I trusted the code that I live by to be truthful and it failed me.

The door opens and Cara stands up. She's dressed just

like you'd see on a television crime show: Black slacks, white button down shirt with a glock resting on her hip. I have no doubt she could kick my ass, but I'd let her win anyway just so she'd have to nurse me back to health.

I step back, realizing that I'm having thoughts of the two of us in compromising situations when I'm not sure I should be. I tried to fight to keep Ryley, but in the end she let me go. I should feel comfortable moving on and maybe I am, but I'm afraid of what might happen if Cara rejects me. Kissing is one thing, but a commitment is another.

"I'm Special Agent Jeffrey Blaine, please call me Blaine."

"I'm SA Cara Hughes with the FBI and this is Senior Chief Petty Officer Nate Archer," she says shaking his hand. I do the same and stand to the side of her. "Thank you for seeing us in Commander Clarke's absence, she's not mobile at the moment."

"No problem," he says, motioning for us to follow him. "I have to tell you that I really shouldn't be talking with you, but Carole asked me to do her this favor." He sits down at a table and we sit opposite him. On the table there are multiple folders and four of them have my brother's team members' pictures, including his. "I've known Carole for a long time and we've worked together before, but never have I been handed a smoking gun like that Blackberry."

Blaine slides one of the folders toward himself and opens it. "As you can see we started a file, one for each of the SEAL Team 3 members who had gone to Cuba. Through our investigation and with the help of the cell phone, we've uncovered a high powered cover-up."

"High powered?" I ask.

Blaine chuckles and shows me a picture. "Do you know

who this man is?" I nod, knowing full well that it's Commander Ingram. "What about this man?" I shake my head, but Cara speaks up.

"That's Lawson. I've been following him for about a year. He's involved in child pedophilia, but I haven't been able to nail him on it yet. When he showed up here I dug a little more, but everything was cold until Evan told me Ingram is Lawson's father."

"But what do they have to do with the Blackberry?" I ask as I become more confused.

"I know this is a sensitive matter and that your family has been through a lot. I wish we had this case years ago, but we understand why we didn't. This is a folder of all the emails that we retrieved from the phone. I'm going to give you both a few minutes to look them over. We'll be making an arrest in the morning. Carole has asked that you inform your brother of what's going on so he knows about the parties involved." Blaine pushes the manila folder to the middle of the table and stands. Before he leaves the room he says, "Hughes, you were right to suspect Lawson. He admits to kidnapping Abigail Chesley, the same child SEAL Team 3 went to Cuba for."

I jump when the door slams, but Cara doesn't as she digs right into the folder. I'm either in shock or completely stunned at what Blaine said before he left. My brother's life was ruined because a Senator had a child kidnapped, but why?

"Why what?" Cara asks as she flips through the mound of emails.

"Huh?"

"You asked why?" Apparently I was speaking out loud and didn't realize it.

"I don't know," I say. "I think it was just a reaction to what

I heard."

"Hmm… look at this. Lawson was having an affair with Vice President Charlotte, but why would he kidnap her daughter?" Her brows furrow as she reads over the emails. I take a stack and start looking through them. None of the names I see mean anything to me and the email addresses are just gibberish.

"Oh god," Cara slumps back in her chair. "Blaine must've told Carole what he found and that's why she wants you to tell Evan." Cara hands me a piece of paper, it's written correspondence that tells us exactly who's involved. I read and then reread the names, words and actions of people we trusted and can hardly believe the words I'm seeing on the page. Names I recognize… of people I know…of people I *trusted*. My stomach turns at the thought of everything my brother has lost at the hands of a friend.

"I need to go see him."

chapter 28
Evan

I HAVE NEVER SEEN SOMEONE so independent, especially with only one arm, as Ryley is. I thought I could help out by being here, but I was sorely mistaken. Everything that it takes me two hands to do, she can do with one and do it ten times better. All that she's done is reaffirm what I've always said about her; she's a warrior.

My warrior.

Being at Ryley's… in our home that we bought together… is exactly where I want to be, except I want to be *with* her. I'm at the point where I don't know if I'm moving a step forward with her or three steps back. This morning she met Nate for breakfast and I'm trying not to act jealous, but I am. He has a hold on her that I can't break through. I know the honorable thing to do is to step away. To let them be together and build a life even if it's not what I want or deserve. I would understand if I had broken up with her, but I didn't. I never wanted to leave her in the first place. I just wanted to do my job and protect our country so Americans don't have to lock their doors at night.

EJ and I have been spending some quality time together. We do everything from watching cartoons in the morning, playing outside, walking Deefur, helping Ryley make dinner, and then me tucking him in at night. Right now that's about my favorite thing to do and it usually takes Ryley waking me to get me out of his bed. He's the best of Ryley and me and I hate that I wasn't here when he was born.

The house is quiet when I return from dropping EJ off at Carole and Jensen's. I remember when I was his age that going to my grandparents' house was the highlight of my life. No rules, tons of junk food and my grandfather had the best train collection. Just thinking about those trains brings a smile to my face and reminds me that I need to ask my mom about them. I know we had them after he passed away and maybe she kept them. I think setting them up with EJ would be good father and son bonding.

Bonding that could lead to him calling me "Daddy". I still hold out hope.

I follow the sound of soft music coming from upstairs. If this were any other time I'd hope she was in the shower and I could join her but even if she is, at best I'll sit on her bed and wait for her to come out. It's hard to accept that the one person you're in love with loves you, but can't be with you. It's even worse knowing it's your own brother standing in the way.

I find her in her bedroom dressed in one of those skimpy tank tops and boxer shorts and surrounded by papers. She's really not leaving much to the imagination and lord knows mine is flying at mock speed to the danger zone. I listen to the music, recognizing the songs I haven't heard in a long time but know just the same. It's our playlist. She's playing songs I put on cd's for times when we had to drown out certain noises, and music that I gave her to listen to before I left.

"What's going on in here?" I ask, pointing to the box and papers all over the floor. She looks up at me with tears streaming down her face. I immediately go to her, dropping to my knees and cupping her face. My thumbs do their best job at wiping away the tears, but the sadness in her eyes is still there.

"Babe, talk to me," I plead. When she shakes her head I sit down next to her and pick up one of the sheets of paper.

Hey Babe,

> *It sucks here. I'm going to tell you the truth because I know you'll listen. But first I'm going to tell you how much I love you and how much I miss you. Okay, back to the suck. It's gross, brown and dirty all the time. I can't believe I'm saying this, but if I never go to the beach again it'll be too soon. Will you still love me if we become people who only go to the Country Club?*

Love, Archer

I pick up one after another, reading the words that I wrote her from basic training, deployments and when I was just miles away from her while she was in college. Letter after letter of my life in detail, written just for her, are spread out on the bedroom floor. I remember everything that I wrote to her, like when my dad died and even though I came home and saw her, I still put it into words because she would listen and I needed to get it off my chest.

Dear Ryley,

> *How are you? I wish I could say that I'm well, but things are hard. Aside from missing you, everything about Afghanistan is hell. Sometimes I wonder how our lives would be different if I had accepted a scholarship to play football or baseball, instead of enlisting. But then I think about how I love serving my country and how I know I'm protecting you and think that I need to kick my own ass for second-guessing my career choice. I know it's only months until I can see you again, but when you break down the hours, it seems like forever.*

I love you, Babe.
Love, Archer

"You kept them all?"

"Yeah. I had them in a box in the attic and something just told me I needed to bring them out."

Hey Babe,

> *I just left your room and can't stop thinking about what we just did. If your father knew, he'd kill me, but damn it if that wasn't the hottest, sexiest moment of my life.*

"This one," I say, holding up the letter. "Do you remember this night?"

Ryley leans into me and looks at the letter. Her breasts brush against my arm and are on full display for my bugged out eyes. I swallow hard and will the sensation growing in my shorts to go away. Tonight is not the night for a serious session of dry humping, even if it's what I want.

"Oh, I remember," she says, leaning into me more instead

of moving away from me.

"Me too. It was my last night home before my orders came in. You still had to graduate so you couldn't come with me. I hated that. We had dinner with your mom and dad, but you had a curfew and I respected that. I truly did. But that night I was sitting in my room thinking about you and I needed you. It wasn't some chance to blow my nut or to just have sex. My body needed yours in a way I can't describe. I was never more thankful for the training I had until that night, when I climbed the tree by your window and landed on your roof without waking your dad.

"You wanted me just as bad. I remember your little whimpers as we kissed and how your back arched off the hardwood floor when I entered you. Making love to you that night was the most intense feeling in my life. I don't know if it was the danger, or fact that our lips never left each other. Every moan, every gasp and every inhale, we shared as one." As I'm recounting this night, her fingers trail over my body. Her fingers trace the outline of my muscles. Goosebumps rise in their wake, making the hair on my arms stand at attention. I look at her and it's a mistake because I want her more than ever. Ryley's eyes are hooded and full of lust. Her bottom lip is pulled between her teeth. It's her sign, and one I am very familiar with. I swallow hard and continue retelling a story that she knows as well as I do.

"I got on that bus the next morning a changed man. I knew deep in my heart that no one would ever compare to you. That no one else would ever own my heart and soul. That night you branded me as yours." The entire time I'm recounting this story, I can't stop staring at her. I silently hope that what I say will remind her how we feel about each other

215

and she will finally make a decision... the *only* decision as far as I'm concerned.

I don't know how much longer I can wait.

"I couldn't believe that we did that, on the floor no less, with my parents down the hall."

I laugh and pick up a few more letters. "I think your dad would still kill me if he ever found out. You should probably hide that letter a little better." I read a few more, each one bringing back a different memory until I can't take it anymore. Sitting next to her and reading about the things I want to do to her is causing a serious problem for me.

"I'm going to go," I tell her as I attempt to stand, but she grabs my hand, holding me in place.

"Don't go."

I shake my head. "Ryley," I say sighing, "it's been a long time since I've been with you and reading these letters, and remembering that night... I just... I *really* need to go." I'm having an internal battle with myself and it's taking everything in me to stop from just putting my heart on the line and telling her how I feel, how I can't take the wait anymore. But if I let my walls down now, will I push her away too soon? As much as I want to stay, as much as I want to be with her, I know I can't push her so it's best for me to leave before I do something I'll end up regretting.

"Can you do me a favor?" she asks quietly, her hand still holding on to my arm.

I want to roll my eyes because she knows that I'll do anything for her, all she has to do is ask. "Anything, babe."

"Choose me."

"Wh... What?" I say, my voice cracking.

Ryley gets up on her knees and places her hands, cast and

all, on my cheeks. "Choose me. Choose EJ. Choose the life we were supposed to have. Choose to live in our house and raise our son together."

"Wait... I don't understand. I thought that you and N—"

Her lips cut off my sentence. All it takes is the gentle brush of her lips across mine, and I'm a mess. I chase her lips, making the kiss more forceful as I work to make my mark on her mouth. I pull her down on me so that she's straddling my lap and push my erection into her flimsy shorts. I hiss as she grinds against me, and the ache in my balls grows increasingly painful. I push her off slightly, and am rewarded with the look of pure need as her eyes travel from mine, to my lips, to the rock hard bulge straining against my shorts, and back again. I've seen this look before, it's the same one she gave me that night in her room, the same one she's given me each time I've returned from deployment or a team mission. But right now, I'm really trying not to rush into anything. Not now. Not our first time in six years.

"Ryley, please," I plead with her. We've had some pretty heavy make-out sessions and one epic dry humping performance, but I'm on the edge about to explode. "I'm not gonna lie, babe, you're so fucking sexy." I grip her hips, digging my fingers into her flesh.

She smiles shyly, biting her lip as she pulls her tank top over her head, giving an absolutely clear sign of what she wants.

"Fucking hell, Ry. You're making this really hard." My words are caught in my throat as she presses down on my erection. The eighteen year old in me returns, remembering the first time we made love. The roles are reversed now with me being unsure. It's been so long, I'm afraid of making a mistake, but if I don't touch her soon I'm going to die. Without taking my eyes off her until I have no choice I kiss along her collarbone until I reach the valley of her breasts.

Ryley leans back slightly, giving me the space I need. My fingers trail over her skin, watching it pebble. Cupping her glorious breasts in my hands, she rocks against me. I lean forward and let my tongue taste her first before pulling her puckered nipple into my mouth. Once I get a taste, it's not enough.

Somehow I manage to pick her up and place her on the bed. She pulls me down to her, kissing me deeply as her legs wrap around my waist. I may know how to make her body respond to me, but it's been years and I think it's time to refresh my memory.

Pulling away, I lean back on knees and stare down at the woman I love. I rub my hand over my erection to ease some of the ache, but her eyes follow my hand and when she sees what I'm doing she licks her lips. I groan at the thought of what she's offering me.

"Ryley Clarke, I have to know. Do you love me?"

"Yes," her voice is sweet, yet husky.

"Do you want to be with me?"

"Yes."

"Only me, now and forever?"

She nods and reaches for me. "Evan Archer, I want you to make love to me."

I pull her hand into mine and realize for the first time that she's not wearing a ring. Her finger is bare and that, to me, means everything. Standing up, I pull my shirt over my head and toss it onto the floor. I flick the buttons on my shorts and pull down the zipper, letting them drop to the floor next. Her nimble fingers tug at my boxers, yanking them down until I'm free of the fabric confines. When she licks her lips, I'm done for.

Pushing her back on the bed, I pull down her stupid little shorts only to find she's naked underneath. "Ry," my voice breaks as she pulls me to her. Flesh on flesh, the warmth of our skin is our only cover. I kiss her deeply as she wraps her legs around me. Our hands intertwine as our hearts beat loudly over the music.

I groan when I feel her wetness coat me and hate myself for what I'm about to say to her. "Never in my life will this happen again, but it's going to take me seconds before I blow. I promise you, I'll make it up to you all night long."

If I didn't love her so much I'd be angry with her for laughing at me, but I'm not. I close my eyes and enter her and just like that night on her bedroom floor years ago, her back arches and her nails dig into my skin. I don't kiss her because I need to hear her whimper, I need to hear the intake of breath that she takes from the pressure between her legs.

Before I can open my eyes, I'm done and embarrassed as hell. After six years of no sex, and two months of blue balls, I'm the master of a quickie. I roll over and cover my face, trying to laugh it off but to no avail.

Ryley tries to sit up, but I'm on the side where her casted arm is. I move to help her, but only proceed in helping her straddle me again. "I heard guys can last longer if the woman is on top," she says as she starts rocking back and forth. That's all it takes for me to be at attention again, that and her glorious breasts bouncing around.

Bringing my knees up to give her some support, I slip into her and use my hands to guide her hips. As much as I love having her on top, I want to feel her body against mine. I want to hold her, kiss her and see her face when I make her feel like a woman again, like the one I fell in love with so many years ago. I want her to see my face when I let go because right now I feel like a new man...

A man who finally has everything he's dreamed of.

chapter 29
Nate

"I DON'T WANT THIS TO be awkward," Evan says, gesturing between us before he hands me a cup of coffee. We're meeting this morning, away from the house and Ryley. What I have to show him, he needs to see without her being in the room. I've hidden a lot of my work from her over the years and while it pains me to hide this, it's for her own protection.

"I agree and I know that things between us are rocky, I can respect that." I take a deep breath and ready myself for what I'm about to say. "I don't know where things are going, if anywhere, with Cara. Seeing her brought back so many memories and made me realize that the love I have for Ryley doesn't even scratch the surface of what I feel for Cara. One look and I was taken back to the day I met her and all the time we took falling in love with each other. I know that's what you feel for Ryley and I should've stepped aside. I'm sorry."

"Apology accepted," he says, but I hold my hand up.

"I'm not done," I say with a shake of my head. "I love EJ.

But I also love Cara and I know in order to have a future with her, if she'll even consider it, I'm going to have to let that part of EJ go. As much as it'll kill me to leave, I need to find some happiness."

"Leave?" he questions.

"Cara has a life away from here. I can't ask her to move but I'm willing to move for her. She came here for me one time in her life, so I would do the same for her. I thought you and I could go to the Clarke's and just spend some time with EJ and let him see that we're brothers and not two men vying for his love."

"All right," he agrees, but I feel as if he's skeptical. I guess I would be, too.

"But before we go, the other reason I wanted to meet you here is because I have some stuff to show you. Yesterday, Cara and I met with Carole's contact at the NCIS." I hold the file folder in my hand. "This shit," I say, shaking my head. "It's deep and it hurts. As your brother, I'm furious this even happened. Someone we know knew you were alive."

Evan's face deadpans as he reaches for the file. I hesitate, but only briefly, before handing it over. "Special Agent Blaine will be making an arrest later this afternoon. Carole asked that you be given the opportunity to confront the people concerned and he's allowing it as a favor to her."

He nods as he opens the folder and visibly stiffens. Cara arranged the documents as such that everything he needs to know is on top. He looks up at me with a mixture of anger and sadness. The realization that someone we trusted took away six years of his life is written all over his face. For the first time since I buried a body I thought was my brother, I'm angry. His pain is mine. We share it. Not only has he lost something, but so has EJ, Ryley, our sister and mother, even the Clarke's. What these people have done is unthinkable and they need to pay.

"Um…" he clears his throat and grips the side of the table.

"This is why I want you to see EJ first. Let him calm you down and remind you of what's at stake. You're just like me and your first thought is that you want to kill them, but not today. I won't let you. You've suffered enough, we all have, and Ryley and EJ need you. *They're*…" I jab at the folder with my index finger, "not worth it. They'll get theirs in the end. I can promise you that."

Evan rubs his hands over his face and yells at the top of his lungs. Bystanders stop and look, but I ignore them. They're lucky that's all he's doing. His leg bounces, a clear sign of agitation and my cue to get him out of here and to a place where I know he's welcomed.

"Come on," I say standing up. "Carole and Jensen are waiting for us." I pick the folder up off the table and tuck it under my arm. Pausing next to his chair, I'm banking on Evan being more like me in the sense that when I'm on edge, when I need to be talked off the cliff, EJ has been the one to do it. I realize now that could've all been because he was my link to Evan, but regardless, I need to try.

I put my hand on his shoulder and squeeze. "Let's go see your son," I say, the word *son* rolling off my tongue easily. Evan stands and slams his chair into the table, causing the other patrons to jump.

The drive over to the Clarke's is a short jaunt from where we are and as soon as we pull in, the garage door opens with Jensen and EJ standing there waving at us.

"I'm not going to stand in the way of you and your son," I say, as I turn off the ignition and exit the car. EJ runs up to me, just like I knew he would. I scoop him up and hold him in my arms.

"Hey buddy." I pull him into a hug and walk us off to the side of the house, giving us privacy and letting Jensen and Evan chat. I squat, setting EJ down on his feet. When I look into his eyes, I see Evan. Everything about this little boy is Evan, aside from his hair, which is a mixture of Evan's dark brown and Ryley's red.

"Remember at the park when you asked about Evan being your dad?"

He nods. "'Cause my name is Eban junior and he's Eban. He kinda looks like me but really look like you." EJ smiles and that alone makes everything right in my world.

I sit down, resting my back against the house. In my head everything works out and what I'm about to say makes sense. But in reality, it probably doesn't and I know I have to tread carefully here. EJ sits in front of me crisscross style and starts picking at the grass.

"So, I wanted to tell you today that I'm going to move to a new house, and it's my hope that Evan moves in with you and your mom."

"Why? Don't you lub me?"

"I do, and I love your mom, but Evan is your dad and he wants to *be* your dad. He wants to take you fishing and teach you how to throw a ball. When we were kids, your dad was one of the best football players in our state and he played basketball and baseball. He just wants a chance to teach you what he knows and to show you that you are the most important person in his life." I look for any sign of resistance or hesitation from EJ and see none, so I continue, "I know it's hard to understand right now, but maybe when you're a little bit older, you'll sit down and talk about everything that happened when you were little."

"Are you still gonna be my dad?"

I don't want to say no, but it's the truth. "I think I can be someone a bit cooler than a dad."

"What?" he asks, full of excitement.

"An uncle... and let me tell you why it's cooler. Being an uncle is the best thing ever because it means I get to do whatever I want and your mom and dad can't say anything about it. And when you're upset, you just pick up the phone and call me and I can help you."

He looks at me with furrowed brows and shrugs. "Are you and mom still getting married?"

I shake my head and point to the garage behind me. "I think your dad wants to marry your mom. He's been waiting a really long time to do that."

"Oh," he says and continues to pick at the grass.

"Maybe you want to go see your dad for a little bit."

EJ stands and wipes off his legs. "Do I have to call him 'Dad'?"

Hearing him ask this breaks my heart, but I shake my head. "Not right now, but I'm sure someday you'll want to."

Evan and I drive in silence. There's tension in the car but it's not between us. For the first time, I was able to witness my brother bond with his son, something that should've happened on the day he was born. After EJ and I had our little chat, the three of us went down to the beach and tossed the football around. I excused myself shortly thereafter and went back to the house and watched the two Evan's have a chance at being father and son.

When we pull up outside the house, Special Agent Blaine is sitting in his car. He nods but stays there, giving Evan a chance to get some answers. Evan stops at the bottom of the steps leading to the house and looks around.

"This is some seriously fucked up shit."

"I know," I say as I pat him on the back, encouraging him to continue. When he gets to the door he knocks and when the door swings open, I place my hand on his shoulder to hold him in place. River is not the enemy.

Evan and I walk in, both taking a seat on the couch, the folder resting in my lap. Evan takes a deep breath and turns his gaze to River who is seated in the chair next to him.

"Where's Frannie?"

River shrugs, knowing that his first instinct is to protect his wife. "She left last night. Said that with us being apart for so long, she grew accustomed to a lifestyle and now that I'm back, she can't deal with it."

I hand Evan the folder and he places it on the coffee table with a thud. I pull out my cell phone and text Cara, letting her know that Frannie isn't here, hoping she'll get the message to Blaine. There isn't a single piece of me of that feels sorry for River right now.

Evan clears his throat and says, "Frannie knew we were alive. She's the one who was sending the care pack –"

"How dare –"

Evan stands, towering over a seated River. I stand, as well, in solidarity with my brother. "No! You listen to me! Your wife knew that we were alive and chose to help her sick, twisted, fucking excuse for a brother. Weeks ago I found a cell phone in the bathroom and turned it over to NCIS. Each email they found is printed out, detailing every aspect of what went down. Registered in your name is a black SUV currently in Mexico for auto body work, the same SUV that tried to kill Ryley and Carole." Evan starts to pace and I put myself between him and River. From everything I've read, River didn't have any clue about any of this and was just the unlucky man who married into this dishonorable family.

"Six years we stayed in that jungle to protect that piece of shit Senator, who, as it happens, is your brother-in-law. We were there because he was having an affair with Christina Charlotte and when it ended, he kidnapped her daughter, raping her repeatedly before sending her to Cuba as a sex slave. Charlotte called her father-in-law, Brigadier General Chesley, and from there, favors were called in and we were sent to get the girl – which we did – but we stumbled onto something huge. When I shot Renato, it sent off a chain reaction."

"Evan, I didn't know."

"How could you not know who your wife's father is?" Evan roars. "He decides when we take a god damn piss."

River looks shaken and confused. He rubs his hands through his hair. "Frannie told me she was adopted. I never asked if she knew her family. I didn't..."

"Your fucking wife kept me from my son," Evan says, adding salt to an already wounded man. "Rask doesn't have a family because of her and who the fuck knows where McCoy's wife and daughter are."

Evan sits back down and holds his head in his hands. "She tried to kill Ryley," he says defeated. "She watched Ryley go through hell, pretending to be her friend and yet she knew everything. She took Ryley's pain and wrote me letters. She wrote you, Rask and McCoy, telling us how we were their heroes and they couldn't wait for us to come home. School pictures, art work and pages from coloring books, all sent by her and for what?"

River shakes his head. "I don't know," he says, as his voice breaks and tears fall down his face. "I thought she was sick. I talked to her about getting help because I had a hard time understanding why everything was exactly how I'd left it, why there was cold beer waiting for me. I'm sorry, Evan."

"You were our leader and she was supposed to be the leader at home, but instead she's destroyed all of us because her brother is a fucking pervert."

"I didn't know," is all he says over and over again. I put my hand on Evan's shoulder, signaling that there's nothing left here for us and that we need to go.

"You were my friend, my brother, but no more. I can't trust you." With those words Evan walks out of the house. I take one look at River before picking up the folder. He never once asked for proof, choosing to believe his fellow SEAL over his wife.

Walking out, I find Cara with her arms wrapped around Evan. There's no jealousy coming from me and I'm thankful she's there to comfort him. When she sees me, she lets him go and greets me with a kiss, making me believe we'll be okay.

"I arrested Lawson this morning and there's an APB out for Frannie right now. The San Diego field team is with Ingram. I know it doesn't make up for what you lost, Evan, but it's a little closure nonetheless."

"Thank you, Cara."

She nods. "The body that was discovered is, in fact, O'Keefe's. We searched his house and found letters that he had written, detailing his part in all of this. He's also the one who wrote the sole article that appeared in the paper. From what we've gathered, he was trying to be the whistleblower but just didn't have the chance to really get it done."

"There *will* be a trial. You'll get your day in court. I'll make sure of it."

Cara kisses me again before climbing into her car. We have family plans later at Evan and Ryley's. Our mom and Livvie will be there, as well as Jensen and Carole. It'll be nice for us all to be together again. We haven't had that in a long time.

Evan and I get in the car, both letting out a sigh of relief. "Where to?" I ask as I pull away from the curb.

"Magoo's," he says without hesitation and I agree with him that we could use a beer right about now. I careen to a stop when a loud boom shakes my car. A quick look in the rearview mirror confirms my worst fears as a fireball projects toward the sky. We get out and run toward River's, but we're too late. The house is fully engulfed in flames and before I can call for help, sirens wail in the background.

chapter 30
Ryley

FOR A LONG TIME I hated coming to the beach because it reminded me of Evan. When he came back to me, he didn't hesitate to bring me out here. At first I was uncomfortable but those uneasy feelings quickly subsided because he was here with me.

Tonight marks six months since everything came to light, since a bomb leveled River's house and Frannie went on the run. My life could be so different right now, but by the grace of God, I'm whole. I hate thinking about what could've been but when I close my eyes or hear the screech of tires, I know that I'm lucky that Evan and Nate walked out of River's house when they did. If they hadn't, EJ and I would be alone right now.

I've had enough *alone* to last me a lifetime.

Evan and I have both been going to therapy and, for the most part, it helps. I have so much anger that I'm not sure I'll ever be able to curb it. Not until Frannie is behind bars. I don't know if that will ever happen, but I hope for my sanity it does. I don't want to always be looking over my shoulder for the rest of my life and, as long as she's out there running around, that's what I'm going to be doing.

The ocean is calm tonight with only the occasional crashing wave. My toes are buried in the sand and my arms are covered with a sweater. I can't decide if I'm hot or cold right now. Evan sits down behind me, surrounding me with his hulking form. Leaning into him, he wraps his arms around my shoulders.

"Are you sad that this is our last night here?"

I shake my head. After everything happened, we decided to sell our house and move back to Washington. Our new place is about a block from the beach, but it's different there. When the Department of Defense got involved, we knew it'd take years before anyone went to trial and we didn't want to wait. The Navy also offered Evan a very nice "please retire and don't sue us" package that was too good to pass up. Besides, he said he's never leaving me again so he really can't be an active member of the military.

It's odd to think that he's retired, though, at such a young age and I don't know how I'm going to deal with him at home all the time but we'll manage... I hope. Evan asked Nate to go into the private security business with him, but Nate hasn't given him an answer. He wants to provide security detail for Washington's finest, or anyone who needs him. He also wants to have the resources to help McCoy search for his wife and daughter.

I have a feeling Nate is planning on asking Cara to marry him, which means he'll be moving to the East Coast once his enlistment is done. He's leaving the Navy too. Nate tells me things, we gossip like high school girls, but it's mostly for advice. We're still best friends, and Evan knows that will never change.

My SEALs, my warriors, have chosen home as their battlefield.

"I'm going to miss my parents, though."

"They won't be far behind us," he says, as he kisses my shoulder. "We can stay until your mom retires, if you want."

"No, I want to be settled before EJ starts school. We'll fly down. Besides, it'll be awhile. She's not ready to quit, not now."

Evan and I sit in a peaceful calm, watching the sunset over the ocean. I am going to miss this, but I think getting far away from Coronado is for the best. I want to put all the bad memories behind us and start over back where Evan and I began.

I shift in his arms, dropping the folded piece of paper I've been holding.

"What's that?" he asks, picking it up from the sand before I can. I place my hand over his and shake my head. "What's wrong?"

"I was going to bury it out here tonight." I adjust so my legs are wrapped around him, so I can look him in the eyes and tell him how I feel. "Before you left for basic, you wrote me a goodbye letter and gave it to Nate. After you came home, he found it and gave it to me. I never read it. I didn't want to because the words wouldn't have any meaning since you were home."

Evan holds the folded square between his fingertips as if he's trying to read the words. Part of me is curious to know what he wrote. Did he tell me to move on? Avenge his death? Did he promise to come home and never leave me?

"Do you want to read it?" he asks.

"No, I don't. I have you so that letter is meaningless and you're never leaving me, so I don't need it anymore."

Evan slants his head and kisses me softly as if he's trying to memorize my lips. When he pulls away, he rests his forehead against mine. "I have an idea," he says as he uses his strength to pull us up. He carries me to the fire he started earlier and once we get there, he taps my bottom and I unlock my legs so I can get down.

"The night I wrote this letter you tried to break-up with me, that's about all I remember. I'm tempted to read it, but that would be morbid and probably bad luck and with us driving to Washington tomorrow, we don't need anything bad happening. So I'm proposing that we burn this so we never have to see it again."

My heart skips when he says propose. I thought for sure he would've asked me to marry him again by now, but he hasn't. He could consider us already engaged and might be waiting for me to throw a date out there. I'm too much of a chicken shit to bring it up because it's possible he's suffering from PTSD and getting married is the last thing on his mind.

I cup my hand over his and smile. "Let's burn it," I say as we toss it into the flame. The paper is old and takes no time to ignite and turn to ash. I like knowing that I'll never know the words that he wrote and I love that he'll never have to say them again.

"Hey," Evan says as I stretch in the passenger seat. I smile and look out the window. We've driven through most of the major cities and almost out of California. As soon as we were off our block I closed my eyes. I couldn't say goodbye to the home we shared, the place where we blossomed as a couple. Even with all the bad, Coronado kept us together.

"I'm sorry, I just couldn't watch as we left. I didn't mean to fall asleep."

"It's okay, babe, but would you mind driving for a while?" he says as a yawn takes over. I nod and he signals, taking the next exit.

Evan pulls over at a convenience store which is perfect because I'm hungry and need to use the restroom. I rush in, praying for no line and am ridiculously pleased when there isn't one. It's the small things in life when you're traveling that mean the most.

When I come out, Evan has his arms full of snacks; candy, chips, cookies and nachos. "I thought you were tired?" I ask as I steal one of his cheese covered nachos.

"I am, but I'm also hungry and you have to be starving."

"Ah you love me," I say, reaching up for a kiss.

"I do," he says with a smoldering look that promises to deliver later. I wink at him as I walk away, heading for the coffee counter. I'm not sure where we are, but the coffee will help keep me alert if he's sleeping.

After everything is paid for and the car is full of gas, we're

234

back on the road. Evan is talking about anything and everything he can think of, mostly about EJ starting school soon and our new house that we've only seen through pictures. When we decided to move, it was a mutual decision and one we didn't think twice about. As much as I love the warm weather of San Diego, it's hard to accept all of the pity from everyone again.

With everything that has happened, the publicity became too much. We couldn't leave our house without someone taking our picture or sticking a microphone in our faces. The media disgusts me really. They were nowhere to be found when Evan and the guys came home, but once Lawson and Ingram were arrested, we were primetime news. After a few interviews, I had enough. We needed this attention when four SEALs returned from the dead, not after the perpetrators were arrested.

It doesn't take long for Evan to fall asleep, leaving me with my thoughts. They're scattered all over the place ranging from: Should I find a job? Is Evan's business plan going to work? Does EJ miss us and is he taking care of Deefur? Is EJ driving them crazy, yet? Does Evan want another child, or maybe two? Before Evan was taken away from me he planned to knock me up every chance he could so he could make his own football team, but with the age gap we'd have with EJ, that's not possible. Not that I'd let him anyway, but another child would be nice.

I know that Evan wants to help Tucker McCoy as well as my mom's contact at NCIS. I know that Evan helping means he might have to leave, but I keep telling myself that it's not a deployment and Evan has free will. He no longer belongs to the military, but to himself. Helping McCoy is the right thing to do especially since Evan has found his happiness. Now it's

McCoy's turn.

The city skyline gives way to vast open land and I try to read each passing billboard to pass my time, but one catches my attention. I look for the exit and take it immediately. There are signs guiding me to our destination. One that Evan will be pleased with, I'm sure.

The dirt lot gives way to bright lights and lots of laughter. I pay the parking attendant and follow the guy with the red flashing light to where I need to park. As soon as I shut off the car it dawns on me that it's dusk and this is perfect.

This will be our moment.

"Evan," I whisper as my lips press against his skin.

"Hmm," he mumbles, leaning into me. There are no words to describe how it feels to have him back in my life and to feel him respond to me the way he does.

"I have a surprise for you, open your eyes."

"Babe, unless you're naked, I don't want to see anything."

"I'm totally naked and in a deserted parking lot ready to get it on." I try not to laugh as he opens one eye and attempts to glare at me. He rubs his hands over his face and yawns.

"How long was I out for?"

"Couple of hours," I tell him. "Look around. I thought we could have some fun. You know, break up the trip."

Evan leans forward and looks out the window. By the rise of his cheeks I know he's grinning from ear to ear. "Damn, EJ would love this."

"I know, but we're here now and there will be plenty of carnivals to take him to when we get to Washington," I tell him as I open the car door and get out. I know he'll follow, just as he knows I'll follow him anywhere. I hold out my hand and wait for him to come around. Our fingers link and it's like I'm transported back to being a teenager, giddy and in love.

I know where I want to go first, and after we pay and purchase our ride tickets I'm dragging him to the death trap, as I like to call it. I hate this ride, but he loves it and there's something that I need to do. And it has to be done on this ride.

"Are you sure about this?" he asks as we get in line. His hand is already holding a bag of cotton candy. I roll my eyes and pray that he doesn't hurl.

"I am. It's a part of us, right?"

"Yes, but we could go to the photo booth and make out, we did that last time too."

"It's not always about making out," I say, shaking my head.

Evan looks completely dumbfounded that I just said that. His head shakes slowly as he says, "I must not be a very good kisser because *I* think it's all about making out. Do I need to practice more?"

"Oh my goodness, will you stop?" I hand the carnie our tickets and take a deep breath. The rickety metal and put-together-in-one-day-Ferris-wheel turns my stomach. Maybe I'm not as brave as I thought, but Evan isn't hearing it.

He stands behind with his hands on my hips and his lips to my ear. "I've got you. I'll always keep you safe," he says as he pushes us forward step by step, never letting me go until the bar locks us in.

"You know I'd be happy walking around. We didn't have to do this."

I nod and bury my face in his chest as we start to move. "I needed to do this," I tell him as he rubs my back. The wheel goes around twice, maybe three times. I don't know because I'm not counting and I'm definitely not looking. But when we stop and his words tell me to look, I know we're at the top.

Sitting up, I look around at the peaceful valley surrounding us. We're higher than some trees and I'm trying not to let that freak me out. I shift slightly and look at him, realizing this is now or never and it really has to be now.

"Evan, will you marry me?"

"What?" he asks choking on his word.

"I love you and we've spent far too many years apart. Six years ago we were supposed to get married and couldn't, but we can now and I want to be your wife. I want to have your babies and grow old with you on our front porch."

The ride jerks and we're moving again. Evan is staring at me with bewilderment in his eyes but hasn't given me an answer. We stop and it's our turn to get off. My heart falls because I thought I had this in the bag. Maybe after being home he's realized that we're just perfect the way we are.

"Hey buddy," Evan says to the operator. "I'll give you a hundred bucks if you put us back up top for the next few minutes." The guy doesn't hesitate and slams our bar down, starting the ride again and stopping us when we get to the top.

"Ask me again," he says, cupping my cheek.

I swallow hard. "Will you marry me?"

"A million times over." He kisses me deeply, cradling my face in his hands as our tongues explore and meld together. My hands clutch at his shirt, pulling him as close to me as I can.

When he pulls away, we're back at the bottom and getting off.

"Thanks, man," Evan says as he hands him the money. "Best thing *ever.*"

"Yeah, I hear that a lot," the guy laughs, pocketing the cash.

"Nah, my girl just asked me to marry her and she ain't even knocked up."

I roll my eyes and slap him in the chest, but he just laughs. Someone yells out that they'll marry him because they are knocked up. I grab his hand and pull him out of the crowd and toward the exit before anyone can try to steal my man.

"Why are we leaving? I want to win you one of those giant stuffed animals."

I shake my head, biting my lower lip. "I just wanted to stop and ride the Ferris wheel so I could ask you to marry me."

"I should've asked you by now."

"No," I say stepping to him. "It was meant to be this way."

We walk hand-in-hand back to the car, stopping every few steps so he can kiss me. He tells me that as soon as we're moved in, he's placing a ring on my finger. I'm not worried about a ring. I just want to be his wife.

"When do you want to get married?" he asks as he shuts the car door. He's going to drive us to a hotel because there's no way we can have sex in the car and we *have* to have sex… now… according to him.

"When my mom can walk down the aisle holding only your brother's arm."

"Next summer?"

I nod. "In Coronado," I say, much to his surprise. "I want to marry you on our beach."

Evan smiles and presses his lips to mine. "You and me on the beach surrounded by our friends and family, sounds just about perfect."

"You make everything perfect, Evan."

He does, at least for me. Meeting this man when I was seventeen was a dream come true and with everything that we've been through, marrying him is like starting a new chapter…

One that I can't wait to write.

Evan's Letter to Ryley

Babe,

I thought about starting this out with something corny like "My Dearest Ryley," but that didn't seem fitting. I love to call you "Babe" and figured if you're reading this, it's because I'm not around to call you that anymore.

You tried to break up with me tonight because you didn't want me to feel like I was being held back. I'm hoping that someday I'll be able to tell you how I feel, in words that will make sense to both of us. Right now, all I can say is that you push me forward. You make me want to be the man you deserve in the future. I say future because you and I will be together, but in the event that we're not I want you to promise me something: I want you to find a man who will take care of you, who will treat you like the princess that you are. I want you to be with a man who puts you first because regardless of my job, you'll always be my #1. Nate will be there to protect you from any asshole who thinks he's worthy.

Ryley, I'm making a promise to always come home to you whether I'm battered and bruised, or knocking on your door because I have 24's of leave. It's not going to matter because a lifetime with you is never going to be enough. I know those aren't my words, but words I learned from you and one of the many movies you made me watch but I still mean every one of them.

You're the love of my life, Ryley... never forget that.

Evan

Evan's Mixed CD for Ryley

98 Degress – I Do Cherish You
N'Sync – I Want You Back
Silk – Freak Me
Babyface – Every Time I Close My Eyes
Backstreet Boys – I Want It That Way
Guns n' Roses – November Rain
Michael Bolton – When A Man Loves A Woman
Bon Jovi – Always
Savage Garden – I knew I Loved You
Trish Yearwood – How Do I Live
Skid Row – I Remember You
Maxi Priest – Close To You
Brian McKnight – Back At One
K-CI & Jo-Jo – All My Life
Sarah Mclachlan – Ice Cream
The Pretenders – I'll Stand By You
Luther Vandross – Here and Now
Shania Twain – From This Moment On
Lonestar – Amazed
Boys II Men – I'll Make Love To You
Bryan Adams – Everything I Do

A note about The Archer Brothers from the Beta reader (and BFF)...

About a year ago, I asked Heidi if she would write me a story. I use the word "asked" lightly because in reality I probably bugged her about it for quite some time. Eventually she agreed but with one proviso – that I give her the characters and a cast list.

Mission accepted, I thought to myself, and about a day later, I sent her a character breakdown with a wish list of what I'd like to see in a story. I had no concerns that Heidi wouldn't be able to deliver – we've all seen her work and what she is capable of - but I did think she'd come back to me with a "WHAT THE HELL?!"

The three main characters were called Nate Archer, Evan Archer and Ryley Clarke. Nate and Evan were twins. Ryley was their love interest. Oh, and they had a dog called Deefur (Dee for Dog - geddit?) You all know what followed.

In Here With Me, Heidi far surpassed my expectations. She gave me what I asked for and multiplied it by a thousand. She gave me two main characters that my heart ached for, that I that I sympathised with, that I wanted to cry with and hug and mourn. She gave me a third character – a missing character of sorts – which I wanted to know more about, who I wanted to hear from.

She gave me a story that I fell in love with.

After Here With Me was published, I went back to Heidi and said to her "You know, that's great and all, but hey, I want to know what happened here and here and here" and literally sent her an email with about 15 different points. Not gonna lie, I thought she would defriend me right there and then with another "WHAT THE HELL?!"

But she didn't. Instead, she answered every single point, and gave me much more on top. She wrote Choose Me.

She gave me such complex storylines that absolutely and completely blew me away. Things that I couldn't even think of in my wildest dreams. Things that literally had me saying to her "What the Hell?". Heidi completely and utterly astounded me with her brilliance with each chapter she sent me. One, in particular, just had a LOT of comments from me and I was literally swooning in each comment I left. That chapter was Chapter 9, and I'm sure you can understand why.

The original brief was "Please can you write me a story about twins who love the same girl but that girl is feisty and sassy and isn't weak".

She gave me Ryley Clarke - a fighter through and through. She IS sassy, she IS feisty and she's made the best of the shitty hand she was dealt.

She gave me Evan Archer - a warrior. He loves his girl and his girl is Ryley. He's spontaneous and outgoing. He loves his country and he fights to protect it. He's loyal and what you see is what you get with him.

She gave me Nate Archer - he's the protector. He loves his brother and he loves Ryley. He made a promise to his brother and he followed that through. He quiet and reserved and he's the thinker, but like his brother he is also loyal. Family is important to him and he'll do anything he can to protect them.

I've previously said that all you Team Evan lovers should prepare yourself for Nate and having read this story, I hope you can see that I was not lying. I thought I was Team Evan, and then I thought I was Team Nate but I can honestly say that I am Team Archer through and through.

Heidi - you gave me all of the above and so much more and all I can say is you took my challenge, you ran with it, you gave it life, you gave it soul and you gave me a whole load of feels with it. So thank you. And thank you for writing the story of the Archer Brothers and sharing it with your readers.

Now, about that deal we had when you send me daily Nate and Evan updates - we still on for that, right...?

My name is Tucker McCoy

Six years ago I went on a mission

And when I returned

My Family was gone

Now that the truth is out there I need to find my wife and daughter

In hopes that they can SAVE ME

The next novel in the Archer Brothers

Coming Soon

acknowledgements

If it takes a village to raise a child, it takes a team to write a novel – at least it did for *Choose Me*. My team is beyond amazing and I really couldn't ask for a better support system to be involved in this novel. Writing about the military, as a civilian, is hard, especially when you're dealing with the emotional aspects of deployment, coming home and the like. Writing the Archer Brothers was an emotional journey that I'm very happy I took. The stories I've heard, and have yet to hear, have and will change my life forever.

Yvette: I want to thank you for being the most understanding, loyal and supportive friend I have ever had. I love that we've been on this journey together for years and we're not willing to slow down.

Traci: Who knew we'd come this far? I'm so happy that you're on my team, in my life and that I can call you my friend.

Amy & Dan: Wow - that pretty much sums up my thoughts. You guys have not only opened your door to me, but your life, and for that I'll be forever grateful.

Art: You are someone I never want to play trivia against, but would gladly be on your team any day. Thank you, from the bottom of my heart, for the countless hours and useful information that you've provided for my novels. I'm forever in your debt.

Audrey, Georgette, Kelli, Tammy, Tammy & Veronica: You ladies sure do know how to make everything right in my world. I really can't ask for a better group of girls to spend my time with.

The Beaumont Daily: You guys rock!
To my family: I know the hours are long, but I do it for you!

And finally to the readers: How you keep up with all the amazing novels being published I'll never know, but you do it, and you do it proudly. If you're reading this, take a moment, smile and pat yourself on the back because you, my friend, are a superwoman… or superman!

Excerpt from
Fighting For Love

by L.P. Dover

Prologue

Shelby

Ten Years Ago

I lost everything today.

My hope.

My faith.

My heart.

All that I had done to protect him didn't mean a single thing now. I left to give him a better life, a chance for him to follow his dreams just like we'd always talked about. Except in doing that, and leaving him in the dark, I condemned myself to a fate worse than I could have ever imagined. It had only been three months since I'd left him, but it felt like it had been a hundred long, agonizing years.

I needed him and I needed him now, to feel his arms wrapped around me—holding me tight—and telling me everything would be okay. *It's not going to be okay.* Especially, when the look on the doctor's face went from hopeful to an outright mask of uncertainty when I told her what was going on. She examined me thoroughly and I gritted my teeth through the pain, trying my hardest to stay positive and calm, but it was no use. The only link I had to the one person I'd given everything up for slowly slipped away from me as each minute passed.

Squeezing my eyes shut, I envisioned in my mind that I was back at home getting ready to have the summer of my life before I left for college. It was supposed to be perfect, just me and Matt enjoying our time by the ocean and being what we were … teenagers. Things weren't supposed to happen like this.

The ever deafening silence in the room made me want to scream. My eyes burned like fire, scorching me from the inside out as I tried to hold back the tears. Was I stupid for still wanting to hold onto hope? That maybe there was still a chance.

This can't be happening to me. It's all just a bad dream. It has to be a bad dream.

Shaking my head quickly, I finally opened my eyes only to be blinded by the fluorescent lights of the examination room. The table felt like a boulder against my back, but I lay there, numb to everyone and to everything around me, silently letting the tears fall. I had to brace myself for what was to come.

Jace and Lexi, who were my two closest friends at Berkeley, both squeezed my hands, bringing me back to reality. Lexi, in her Hello Kitty pajamas and her blonde hair in a messy ponytail, tried to stay strong for me, but I could tell she was barely hanging on by a thread. Jace was a different story. He was literally the strong one out of the trio both—literally and physically—however, even the strongest ones broke at times. I could see it in his melancholy, crystal blue gaze that he was also trying his hardest to stay strong.

It all happened when we were studying together in my apartment, eating pizza like we always did for the past few Wednesday nights, when something went terribly wrong. I'd had a few issues before, but everything came back normal after the tests, so I thought I was in the clear. I didn't understand why it was happening again.

Jace and Lexi rushed me to the emergency room as fast as they could, hoping that I'd be okay like I was before. This time was different, though; I could feel it in my blood and I could sense the spark of life dying inside of me as each second passed. A person knows when something is wrong, and I knew something was terribly wrong.

I was so angry with myself that I couldn't even look at my friends without feeling ashamed of how weak I was. I did everything right, and everything I was supposed to do to keep myself healthy and strong. *What more could I do?*

Lips trembling, I bit down hard, not even caring about the pain or the metallic taste of blood on my tongue, and turned my head away. Jace brushed the tears off my cheeks with the pad of his thumbs, but as soon as he did, more fell in their place. It was hopeless.

Putting his forehead to mine, while his other arm wrapped gently around my shoulder, he leaned in and whispered in my ear, "We're here for you, Shels. I texted your mother and she said she'll be down here soon. You're not alone, okay? I'll stay in here with you if you want me to."

"Same here," Lexi agreed, putting her arm around me as well. "I'm not going anywhere either."

Swallowing hard, I nodded quickly, and squeezed my eyes shut. "Thank you," I whispered hoarsely, trying to hold onto their warmth. I was cold, my body trembling and teeth chattering as I tried to take in a deep breath.

Out of the corner of my eye, I saw Dr. Jacobs place her stethoscope on the desk before hesitantly turning toward me with sorrow-filled eyes. "What did I do wrong?" I asked her. Hearing the sound of my voice, I could barely recognize the strangled cry that left my lips. I was heartbroken, and I felt … empty. I guess it was because I was.

She swallowed hard and took a deep breath, approaching me slowly. Her strawberry blonde hair was smoothed back in a tight bun, and even with her glasses on it still didn't hide the turmoil in her midnight blue eyes.

"You didn't do anything wrong, sweetheart," she answered soothingly, placing her hand gently on my arm. Her lips quivered when she tried to reassure me with a smile, but it only added to the grief. "Sometimes it just happens and there's nothing you can do to prevent it. It doesn't mean that it will always happen like this. You're young and healthy. One of these days, when the time is right, it will happen again. I've been through it, too, so I know the pain you must be feeling. The last thing you need to do is blame yourself. It's not your fault."

I nodded quickly, but nothing was going to take away the pain of my loss … of both of my losses. Was it karma rearing its ugly head and taunting me for making the wrong decisions in life? Could it honestly be that cruel to make me pay with such a high price? The desolation and despair I felt in my chest was like a blunt-edged knife burrowing deep into my soul, ripping me from the inside out. I honestly felt like I would die from the torment because it was so overpowering; it was as if the shadow surrounding me sucked away every ounce of happiness I had ever felt.

How can I go back to the way things were?

The answer was simple … I couldn't.

Chapter 1

Shelby

Present Day

There were times in my life when I'd just sit and wonder ... wonder what my life would've been like if I'd stayed and followed my heart; if I'd done things differently. I knew I wasn't the only person in the world who felt regret, but what I wanted to know was why did I feel so alone? I had everything I could ever want, and yet it still wasn't enough. Would it ever be enough?

"Shelby, what are you doing here? I thought Bryan told you to take the day off? Not to mention, I figured you'd be hung over after last night's festivities," a voice from behind me scolded playfully.

Ah yes ... last night. My boss, Bryan Winters, did tell me to take the day off, but I hadn't had one in so long I forgot what they felt like. After winning two National Journalism Awards and getting a promotion, I definitely deserved to celebrate. However, I think I over did it with one too many martinis and getting a little too comfortable with a guy I met at the after party.

Gazing out of my office window at the San Francisco Bay, I didn't have to turn around to know it was Lexi Martin, my headstrong best friend and other half for the past ten years. I could see her reflection in the window, and like always, she had her bright blonde hair pulled back into a ponytail with her Nikon camera securely wrapped around her neck. She never went anywhere without taking pictures of something. There were more pictures of us in college than there were of me as a child.

With a sly expression on my face, I peered at her over my shoulder and replied, "Lex, you know I practically live here at the office. Besides, Jace fixed me one of his cure all smoothies this morning so I feel fine. I guess his studies in Nutritional Science paid off. Anyway, it takes a lot more than that to get me down."

I really need to figure out what he puts in those drinks, I thought to myself as I turned back to the window.

Jace Harding was one of my closest friends and currently sharing a house with me now that Lexi had moved out to live with her fiancé. I thought it would be a little difficult explaining Jace to the guys I dated, but once I told them he was gay it all worked out just fine. It wasn't like I went on many dates, anyway. Jace and I had lived together for the past nine years, and not only was he a wonderful friend, he was family; more like the protective brother I never had since I grew up an only child.

Sometimes I hated not having any siblings. Lexi had a younger sister she was close to, and for that I envied her. They always spent time together, and had a bond that I would never have. Maybe that was a reason why I focused mainly on work and not relationships; work was my significant other.

Staring at my reflection in the window, it was hard to believe that my face now appeared in every issue of the prestigious, *Physique Sports and Fitness Magazine*. In college, all I ever wanted was to work for a prominent magazine and I got my wish. The only thing about my success with *Physique* was that the articles I wrote and became well known for were under my pen name, Paige Monroe. For some reason, I didn't think Shelby Dawson sounded marketable so I changed my name and my whole appearance in the process. It felt good being someone else for a change. Most people at the office usually called me Paige so in a way it felt like I lived a double life. Only Lexi and my boss called me by my real name.

If I was going to be someone else I might as well play the part, right?

My shoulder-length hair was no longer a dull shade of ashy brown—like it was for all of my life—instead, it was now a dark, chocolate brown with honey highlights that matched the color of my eyes. It was also longer in length, which worked great to throw it up into a messy bun on those lazy days.

I graduated from Berkeley with a journalism degree, earning numerous awards among my peers, which happened to get me noticed by the right people. Three weeks after graduating, I found myself in a swank office with a wonderful view and doing what I loved. In the process, I was able to bring Lexi along with me so that she could put her photography skills to good use for my articles.

To get my attention, Lexi tapped her fingers on my desk and cleared her throat. "Hey, no amount of spacing out is going to get you off the hook of giving me details. You never called to tell me what happened between you and Caleb last night. You know Hayley brought him specifically to the party to meet you, right?"

Wide-eyed, I quickly turned around and gasped in disbelief,

"What? I had no idea."

Lexi smiled, batting her eyelashes innocently at me, but she wasn't fooling me; I knew that look. Her and her fiancé, Will, have tried numerous times to set me up with some of his friends, but none of them interested me. They were all arrogant and completely self-involved, and most of all they were boring. Somehow, it didn't surprise me that Hayley wanted to try next.

Hayley was Lexi's younger sister by only two years, and a dance choreographer with numerous music videos under her belt. Her parents made her visit me and Lexi at Berkeley in hopes that we would convince her to go to college instead of pursuing a career in dancing. Hayley had always been headstrong and determined to get what she wanted, so it was no surprise that after high school she followed her dreams against her parents' wishes. She had guts, and I loved that about her.

Crossing my arms at the chest, I glared at Lexi and sighed. "She didn't want to tell me because she knew I would get pissed if she brought a blind date to my party, right?"

Sheepishly, Lexi slumped down in her chair. "Yeah, kind of. She was almost positive you would like him, so she offered me two tickets to see One Direction in concert if I added her boyfriend and Caleb to the after party list. It worked out great, didn't it? He's cute and you both seemed to hit it off pretty well. Since you didn't know it was a blind date, there wasn't all of that blind date awkwardness that you hate so much."

Yeah, that's true, but it could've also been the martinis that helped.

"And you never answered my question," she stated impatiently. "What happened between you and Caleb?" She sat at the edge of her seat, her eyes twinkling with mischief, as if I was going to tell her some big secret. Sadly, there wasn't too much to tell.

"We just kissed, Lexi. That's it, I promise," I replied, taking a seat at my desk and grinning from ear to ear. "He also gave me his number."

Caleb was a great guy; the first man in a long time that actually made me laugh and smile. I had a good time with him, flirting and talking, and once the night was up I let him kiss me goodnight. He left the ball in my hands by giving me his number, so it was only a matter of calling or not calling him. However, underneath that carefree attitude of his and boyish smile, I couldn't get over the color of his majestic, emerald green eyes. That color haunted me because they were the same hint of green as the guy I left ten years ago. It was almost like I could never escape the memories of my past.

"Well, are you going to call him?" she asked excitedly.

When my smile faded, Lexi sighed and reached for my hand across the desk. Over the past few years I'd dated different men and I actually slept with a couple of them, thinking that the intimacy would help me move on. I was twenty-seven years old; I wanted a long lasting relationship. So far nothing had worked.

"Shels, you need to stop this. Moving on isn't easy and I understand that, but if you don't honestly *try* to then it's never going to happen. Whether you call Caleb back or not, you owe it to yourself to be happy. You can't punish yourself forever. You *are* worthy of a relationship, you know."

Her words were the truth, but it didn't stop my heart from wanting to hold onto the past just a little while longer. There was always that part of me that said, *Don't give up, there is still hope.* I'd been saying that for ten years and nothing ever came of it. You could only hold out for so long before life passed you by. *Do I honestly want to waste more time?*

The answer was no.

Hanging my head and closing my eyes tight, I blew out a

shaky breath and finally found the courage to admit my secret, "You're right, Lexi. I have been punishing myself by holding onto the past, but the truth is that I don't know how to move on. I can't seem to let go."

Squeezing my hand, Lexi breathed a sigh of relief, and with a smile on her face, uttered happily, "Well, it's about damn time you admitted you have issues. That's the first step to moving on. Why don't you call Caleb and hang out as friends? Take things slow and see where it leads. It doesn't hurt to see what could be there."

Getting to her feet, she adjusted the camera around her neck and ambled toward the door. "All right, now that I've given you a day's worth of good advice, I have to go. If you know what's good for you, you'll take the day off and use that time wisely." She stopped by the door and turned around, gazing out the window behind me with a sly grin on her face. "You know, it's a beautiful day out there. A day at the beach would be the perfect time to relax and get to know someone without the pressure of other people around. Just saying …"

She winked at me and disappeared out the door. It didn't take a genius to figure out what she was suggesting, so the only issue was if I was going to heed it. Staring at my computer screen, an email from Bryan popped up, but instead of opening it up I turned off my laptop. Today was supposed to be my day off, so I was going to treat it like one. If Bryan's email was important it would be in my inbox tomorrow morning. For now, it was my time to let it go and enjoy a day at the beach.

It was going to feel good to do something different, and it was only the beginning.